# Gentleman and the Witch

## The Grae Sisters
### Book Three

## Eve Langlais

Copyright © 2023 Eve Langlais

Cover © Addictive Covers

Produced in Canada

Published by Eve Langlais

http://www.EveLanglais.com

E-ISBN: 978 177 384 4824

Print ISBN: 978 177 384 4831

**ALL RIGHTS RESERVED**

This book is a work of fiction and the characters, events and dialogue found within the story are of the author's imagination and are not to be construed as real. Any resemblance to actual events or persons, either living or deceased, is completely coincidental.

No part of this book may be reproduced or shared in any form or by any means, electronic or mechanical, including but not limited to digital copying, file sharing, audio recording, email and printing without permission in writing from the author.

# Foreword

On my sixteenth birthday, I became a witch.

Kind of cool, I won't deny, although I could have done without the bullshit that came along with it—getting my period at school being the worst. I'd worn a skirt that day, and the blood rolling down my leg had me fleeing for home as fast as my blocky heels could take me.

Unlike my sisters, I didn't consider it the most pivotal day in my life. I wasn't impressed with the puny magic I suddenly acquired. So what if I could light a candle with a snap of my fingers or cause that annoying twat, June, to trip and fall flat on her face after she tried hitting on my boyfriend? Raining outside and a red light kept

## Foreword

me standing there getting soaked? Easy peasy to change it to green and get a snicker out of the cars slamming on the brakes and sliding to a stop.

Parlor tricks. So why mention them? Because I didn't resent my lack of true ability until my fiancé died of cancer. Despite my power, I couldn't save him or do a damned thing to ease his suffering. I felt useless and worried it would happen again.

That impotence led to me looking deeper into the origin of magic. Surely I could learn to do more? To my surprise, I discovered a parallel world known as the arcane that encompassed those with power, like me and my sisters, as well as those classed as nonhuman. Nothing like having your whole existence shaken by the realization monsters did exist.

Not that I became a fighter. That was my sister Enyo's job. Frieda was the one who could see the future, whereas I remained a puny witch until the day a portal opened and my powers got a boost. Suddenly, I could do incredible things. Float like a superhero. Cast fireballs. Open portals to other worlds...

Which leads me to the present. Single, pow-

## Foreword

erful witch who just helped cast a great evil out of the world. Awesome, right?

Not really, because I had to return to my boring life. What a waste of my abilities.

Was it too much to ask for some kind of calamity that would offer a challenge? Oh, and while I'm on the subject of wishes, I could use a man in my life—and bed—because it was getting expensive, not to mention bad for the planet, replacing my overused vibrators.

# 1

The phone rang, and given I had caller ID, I answered, "What do you want, French fry? Shouldn't you be banging your new husband right about now?"

Frieda, my sister—who hated the nickname French fry—had chosen to take up residence in Britain, of all places, putting her about six hours ahead.

"One, we make love. Two, it's only nine o'clock. And three, you might want to stay inside today."

I glanced out the window to see sunny skies. "It's a gorgeous day, and Jinx needs a walk." Jinx being the love of my life, a temperamental

Pomeranian who only loved me—which I was totally fine with.

"If you leave, you are going to become embroiled in something life-altering," my sister warned.

"Really?" Well, that might be a nice change. Ever since I'd returned from my trip abroad, I'd been bored. More so than usual. What was the point of having inherited all kinds of magic only to have nowhere to use it?

"I see danger ahead for you," Frieda added.

"Sweet."

"You sound just like Enyo when I try to caution her about her choices," Frieda complained.

My sister could see the future and often used it to nag us. You'd think after almost four decades of knowing each other, she'd have learned we didn't like the easiest road. I wanted a challenge, whether it be in business or pleasure.

"Excuse me for craving some action."

"That action might get you killed," she grumbled.

"Now you're talking. Is this the kind of danger I can blast to bits?" I'd been practicing my aim, seeing as how I'd recently had reason to invoke combat magic. I dared anyone to tell me it wasn't awesome that I could shoot lightning from my fingertips.

"I swear, I don't know why I bother." Frieda sighed.

"Admit it, you called because you miss me."

"Miss what? You bullying me to leave the apartment? Mocking my clothes? Telling me a dozen times a day to get laid?"

"You whine, and yet look at you now. Living in a different country, getting railed on a daily basis. The only thing you still need to work on is your wardrobe." How I had a sister who thought it was okay to match flowered leggings with a striped shirt was beyond me.

"I see you're going to be contrary, so I'm going to hang up now, but with just one more caution for you to ignore. Keep in mind that evil sorceresses who try to rule the world often end up dead."

"Do you think I could be evil?" I asked, perusing myself in the mirror by my main door. I wore a cute jogging outfit—not that I jogged—in a light pink with "Juicy" spelled out in glittery letters across my butt.

"Aren't you already?" was her sour reply.

My lips curved. "No, but I could be."

"I don't know why I bother. Bye. Oh, and say hi for me."

Before I could ask "Say hi to who?" she'd severed the connection, but I didn't mind. According to her, today was about to get interesting.

"Jinx!" I called my dog, who, of course, didn't deign to reply. She really hated it when I treated her like a dog. Apparently, she thought herself above not only her own kind but humans too.

I found her in my bedroom, lying atop my pillow, shedding hair on it. Every night I changed the casing for it lest I choke on a strand. It had happened before, usually at three a.m.

My dog didn't look at me, the human who dared interrupt her nap.

I crooned, "Does baby want to go for a walk?"

*Boing.* My dog sprang to her feet, her poufy body hiding her short legs. Her tail wagged frantically as she smiled. Yes, smiled. Jinx did love her walks.

"Let's put a harness dress on. What do you think, polka dots or flowers today?" I had several drawers in the front hall dedicated to outfits for my dog, from adorable frothy dresses to a rubber-ducky-covered raincoat with matching booties. Jinx eschewed my suggestion of a very bright red halter dress with matching leash and chose instead a pink vest studded with rhinestones. Despite the sun, the fall weather had arrived with a sharp wind, so I wore a warm sherpa coat and ankle-high black boots. Like I said, I don't jog.

We exited the apartment building to bright sunshine, my sudden squint making me wish I'd brought my sunglasses. I breathed in the fresh air of the outdoors, marred by the distinctive reek of cigar smoke. Rare nowadays, given most people had moved to vaping.

A glance showed a figure in a pea coat over slacks, with neatly coiffed hair and a freshly shaven jaw. The gentleman cut a rather elegant figure, though, and had to be new to the neighborhood since we'd never met. Yes, I was nosy enough to want to know who lived on my block. Annoying people were subtly encouraged to move, like that shrill priss who used to live across the street and thought she could lecture me on the joys of veganism. She crossed a line when she started in on my beloved Jinx, claiming some bullshit about pet ownership was akin to slavery and should be abolished. She even dared to unclip the leash and tell my dog to run free.

At the time, a less-than-impressed Jinx

glanced at me, and I'd shrugged and said, "Your choice, baby." Baby chose to chase the annoying twat before returning to me with a smirk. Slave my ass. If anyone held the upper hand in our relationship, it was my dog.

Given that neighbor didn't learn her lesson and kept haranguing, a few minor spells led to her breaking her lease early. I wondered if it was the roaches or the food constantly rotting in her fridge that led to her snapping.

The gentleman standing at the bottom of my stoop smiled in my direction and my tummy fluttered. What a handsome specimen. He had a matching sexy, deep voice too. "Lovely afternoon, isn't it?"

The weather. The inane conversation starter used by people around the world. "We don't have many left before winter."

"Indeed, we don't, Ms. Grae."

I stiffened. "Excuse me? How do you know my name? Who are you?" My suspicious side immediately wanted to know because this was obviously no chance encounter.

"Not going to guess?"

"I don't play games."

"No, you're usually very direct. A commendable trait."

"You speak as if you know me."

"Because I do. You and I are closely linked."

At that claim, I snorted. "What kind of lame line is that? I don't know you."

"True, and yet that doesn't negate the fact you and I are bound. As are your sisters."

The mention of my siblings had me narrowing my gaze. "Is this your way of saying you're my daddy?" I eyed him up and down. "Damn, you must have been a toddler when you impregnated Mom."

His brows rose. "I am not your father."

"Is what Luke wishes Vader had said," I mumbled.

"What? Who is this Luke?"

The way he spoke niggled at me. Like, who didn't know the infamous Luke and that line from the movie? Somebody who'd not been exposed to any kind of media. Which was impossible if you lived anywhere on Earth these days, unless... "Are you going to keep playing word games, or are you going to tell me who you are?"

"Can't you guess?"

I crossed my arms.

"I'm the god of monsters, but you may call me Typhon, seeing how you are going to help me retrieve my magic."

I blinked at him then took my time sizing him up. Tall, well over six feet I realized. I stood on the stoop and still wasn't eye-to-eye with him. Broad of shoulder, clean-shaven, impeccably dressed. Had to admit, he cleaned up nice. The last time I'd seen Typhon we were in Ariadne's throne room, and he wore a billowing cloak that covered him head to toe, concealing his face.

"You don't look like the god of monsters. Aren't you supposed to have several heads?"

"I can take a monstrous shape if needed, but given humans are easily frightened, this form tends to cause fewer problems."

I cocked my head. "How do I know you are who you say you are?"

He arched a brow. "Do you often have men introducing themselves as gods?"

"Yes," I pertly replied. Then I added, "Usually, they're claiming to be a god in the bedroom."

"In my day, people didn't pretend lest a true god smite them," he grumbled.

"Welcome to the modern age."

I went to step past him, and he growled. "Where are you going?"

"To walk my dog." A dog who'd not barked at him, as she normally did with strangers. On the contrary, Jinx acted like a little lady, standing by my side, looking aloof and adorable.

"I'm not done speaking with you."

"Then make an appointment. I'm busy."

"I'd hardly call walking a mongrel busy."

"Excuse me, I'll have you know Jinx is a purebred Pomeranian. Her parents were show dogs. She's got an impeccable pedigree."

His lip curled. "She's barely snack sized."

"Talk about eating my dog one more time and I won't be responsible for what happens," I snapped. I didn't tolerate insults about me or my sweet dog.

"Exactly what do you think you can do? I'm a god."

"Former god. Given you haven't regained the power Ariadne stole from you, you're barely a step above human."

That brought a mighty glower to his handsome face. "You are trying my patience."

"And you're wasting my time," was my sassy reply. I wiggled my fingers, meaning to teach him a lesson, but rather than giving him a super wedgie, I found my thong riding up my ass crack. Ouch.

My lips parted. "What just happened?"

He smirked. "Have you already forgotten whose blessing you carry?"

My lips pinched, mostly because I didn't want to admit it had slipped my mind that, technically, my magic came from him. It could be confusing, seeing how my mother filched my and my sisters' power from Ariadne, who, in turn, had stolen her magic from the monster god.

What I'd not known until now was my magic couldn't be used against him. "Is this your way of saying you're immune to me?"

"Is that a problem?" he asked in that deep voice of his.

I wanted to say yes, but in actuality, this was kind of interesting. A man I couldn't punish or magic into obeying. But the fact he could fuck with my powers did leave me with an interesting question. "If I can't use your own blessing against you, then does that mean Ariadne can't either?" Ariadne being the twatwaffle I'd recently gone up against with my sisters. She'd escaped into some portal to another world rather than give back what she stole.

"Correct. So long as I'm stuck with this"—he pulled loose his tie and undid the top button of his shirt to show me a metal collar around his neck—"she has access to my powers, but can't use my magic against me."

The ugly thing gave me a chill. I couldn't imagine what it would be like to be cut off from my source of power. To have someone siphon it from me, making me weak.

"Well, at least you don't have to worry about her anymore. She's gone."

"For now. She will return to finish what she began, unless we find her first." His ominous prediction was a reminder that Ariadne planned to kill the monster god and permanently take his power.

"Sounds like a you problem."

"Don't be so sure of that. We are bound, you and I."

I laughed. "No, we're not. And I can prove it." With my chin lifted, I walked away, because if there was one thing self-important people hated, it was being ignored.

# 2

## Typhon

THE DISRESPECT BOGGLED THE MIND. Here was a woman who'd been gifted part of his magic, who bore his mark—making her his to order around—and yet she ignored him. She sauntered off, her heart-shaped buttocks swinging, with that ridiculous poof ball she called a dog.

Walked away from a god.

He scowled before taking long strides to catch up. "Where do you think you're going?"

"To the park. Jinx needs her walk, don't you, baby?" She offered a sweet smile to the hairy rat on a leash.

"We were in the midst of a conversation."

"Which I ended because it bored me. Now run along."

She should count herself lucky he lacked his powers or, in that moment, he would have smote her. "We are not done. Far from it. You will assist me in dealing with Ariadne."

"I already did. Ariadne is gone from this world. Yay. And you're welcome."

"She took my power with her," he reminded her.

"Which I already said is a you problem," she countered.

"She will return which is why it's imperative we find and stop her."

That made the witch pause, and she cast him a sidelong glance. "Will she come back? I mean, she fled because my sisters and I were about to whoop her ass."

"Ariadne will want revenge."

"Ooh, sounds exciting."

He stared at her wondering about her sanity, liking her attitude while hating it at the same time.

She smiled. "What? I'm bored. Who knew fighting an evil twat would be so energizing? I kind of hope she comes back so I can really fuck her up."

"You might have taken Ariadne off guard, but she won't be so easy to defeat the next time," he warned.

"Again, assuming she returns. Could be the place she fled to is nice."

"Doubtful. The pleasant worlds would never allow someone like her to stay."

"But you have no way of knowing for sure. Could be she's stuck like you were."

A reminder that he'd been imprisoned in a barren dimension, a victim of betrayal, until recently.

"I highly doubt she went somewhere she can't escape."

"Says the guy who was stuck for... how long?"

"Only because she cursed the only exit." He felt a need to defend himself.

"Whatever. I don't know why you'd assume she went somewhere shitty."

"Because there are few dimensions closely aligned to ours that are easy to slip in out and out of."

"How many is a few?" she asked.

"Maybe five or six. But most of them she'd have ignored. Like Tartarus—"

"The prison for gods," she interrupted.

"Actually, it is the home of the titans, who happen to be the only ones who are any good at keeping gods incarcerated. I can't see her going there. Nor would she have gone to Elfenland."

"Never heard of it."

"It used to be the home of the fae."

"Why used to be?"

"The fae played with things best left alone, leading to their near extinction. The only ones that remain alive were those who fled."

"Okay, so she didn't go to Elfenland. You said there were a few. Surely not all of them are shit?"

"I doubt she went to Hades."

"Wait, there's an actual Hell?"

He snorted. "Yes, but it's not a place where souls go when they die but rather a hot cesspool for demons."

"Does this mean there's a Heaven too?"

"Heaven is a place of endless skies and clouds, with the only solid place being the Garden of Eden, a dangerous locale where even the most beautiful flower is deadly. Not a place Ariadne would go, just like Nullarcana, a dimension that hates magic and hunts those who have it. They're the ones who created this collar." He tapped it.

"Doesn't sound like she'd be staying in any of those places. But from the sounds of it, there are more."

"There are two planes similar to Earth, but they are very proactive about preventing intruders, so she'd have avoided those."

"Assuming she knew where she went."

"Oh, she knew," was his dark response. "She most likely planned her escape well in advance."

"I wonder if she knows what world she dumped my mom in."

"Most likely yes, since she can't just open a portal to nowhere," he remarked. He'd been there when Ariadne tried to thin those fighting against her by opening a doorway and shoving the triplets' mother through.

"What are the chances she sent my mom somewhere nice?"

"Doubtful, but I wouldn't worry about Apate," he murmured. Apate, the triplets' mother, being the goddess of deceit and powerful in her own right.

"What's that supposed to mean?"

"Just that your mother is very resourceful."

"You speak as if you know her."

"Before my incarceration, we were acquainted."

Deino's lip curled. "Oh gross, you slept together."

He couldn't help but laugh. "No. We are friends, nothing more."

"Seems like more than friends. After all, she had triplets for you and even had the balls to steal some of your magic from Ariadne to give to us."

"This is more a case of like sticking together. We are both gods. Ariadne is not. She is a thief. A pretender. She can't be allowed to succeed."

"I hate to break it to you, but hasn't she already? I mean you were imprisoned how long?"

His lips pressed flat. "I am aware of the shame. My weakness is no excuse."

"How much of your power does Ariadne have?"

"A good portion of it. But not all. I still have dribbles. You and your sisters have some too."

She eyed him before saying, "If we're carrying your magic, why haven't you taken it back to strengthen yourself?"

He put a hand to the collar at his throat. "So

long as I wear this, Ariadne will just take anything you give me."

"Are you sure you don't want Frieda to try and remove it? Heck, I'll give it a shot if you want."

He gave a violent shake of his head. "No. Given Ariadne is no longer on this world, I don't know what will happen. Could be it severs my power permanently, kills me, or the snap of it could cause an explosion."

"Or is that what she wants you to think so you don't try to remove it?" she countered.

"This parasite metal isn't from this world. I don't know how it will react and, as such, would prefer to not take a chance. I didn't survive my incarceration to die from being rash." He noticed during their conversation and stroll they'd reached a park. The dog didn't seem impressed by the other canines or the grass.

"So you want to find Ariadne to sever the contact between you hopefully without rebound."

He inclined his head. "When your sister released Bacchus from his collar, he didn't seem to suffer ill effect, so I am hopeful." Bacchus being Ariadne's husband, a god who'd also had his power stolen.

"I still can't believe he jumped into that portal after my mom." Her nose wrinkled.

"They were lovers before he met Ariadne."

"Frieda says you banged Ariadne too." Deino glanced at him from under lashes.

He winced. "Not one of my finer moments. Blame a weakness of the flesh."

"Fair enough. I get it." She crouched to talk with her dog in the stupidest voice. "Okay, little sweet baby, you go do a tinkle, and if you do a number two, I've got a treat for you."

"What are you doing?" he asked with a hint of incredulity.

"Cheering on my favorite girl so she'll do her business outside instead of on my shag." She continued singing in that strange, high-pitched voice.

"You let your dog rule you." His mouth rounded. "A thing not even the size of your head."

"Excuse me? My head is not that big."

He glared at the dog. "You." He pointed. "Defecate."

The fluffy creature stared at him.

He stared back.

This was embarrassing. The god of monsters shouldn't be losing a battle of wills with a dog.

"We are wasting time. We need to find Ariadne," he growled.

"What's with this 'we' shit?" she grumbled.

"You're going to help."

"Pretty sure I'm not."

"Your mother owes me."

"And? That's her. Not me, or my sisters."

"She had you for that express purpose."

Her expression tightened, and a hard glint entered her gaze. "I am aware Mother didn't have us out of some maternal instinct. I don't need you shoving it in my face. And it also changes nothing. I don't owe you shit."

Frustration built inside him. There was a time when no one dared speak to him so disrespectfully. The witch saw him as weak. Less than a man. She wouldn't help without the right motivation.

He couldn't think of many things that would get her to change her mind. Threatening her sisters would be the quickest but could also backfire, as she was the type to plot vengeance. So what else might sway her?

"Help me and I will give you even more power."

She eyed him. "I already have quite a bit."

"But not enough to be immortal."

He knew he'd surprised her by the slight stiffening of her body. She was careful not to show too much interest. "Immortality won't help if I'm dead before I get it."

"But if you succeed..." he teased.

"What are the odds of that?"

"I don't know. However, the fact Ariadne fled rather than fought indicates she's fearful we'll manage to defeat her."

"Or she's gone somewhere she can shore up her defense and pick us off if we come for her."

"The quest will be dangerous." He wouldn't lie about that.

"Not exactly a selling point."

"If Ariadne returns before we find her, she will want vengeance on those who thwarted her," he warned.

"Meaning me and my sisters." She looked away before asking, "How are we supposed to handle her if you don't know where she went?"

"There are ways of finding out."

"Let's say we do find her. She still has your magic, and while she might not be able to blast you to kingdom come, she won't have a problem eradicating me."

"If we can separate her from the armband that is linked to my collar—"

"Oh, just that?" she sarcastically retorted. "Easy peasy. Let me get right on that."

"It won't be simple, but your sister achieved it with ease for Bacchus."

"Then why aren't you asking her for help?"

"Alas, the journey we must embark upon is better suited for someone of your skills."

Her gaze narrowed. "Who says I want to travel? Not to mention, you're assuming I can replicate what Frieda did. Need I remind you that my sister acted in a moment of panic with no clue what she was doing?"

"A good thing you are the levelheaded sister who will practice ahead of time."

She stared at him. "Practice how? You told me I couldn't take off your collar."

"There are other objects of magic you can attempt to drain." The armband his collar controlled could only be removed by siphoning the magic holding it in place.

"You've got an answer for everything."

"Of course, I do. I am a god after all."

Her laughter rang out bright and cheerful and oddly pleasant despite the situation.

She shook her head. "You are something, Typhon. Let's say I agree, how do I know you won't go back on your word once you're the monster god again? Who's to stop you from killing me instead of paying up?"

At times he wished he had that kind of dishonor. "I can only give my word."

"Trust isn't something I give to just anyone."

"Understandable, but I will mention, as someone who was betrayed, I would not ever do the same. If I want you dead, I will tell you so."

"Gonna warn me before the smiting?"

His lips twitched. Surely, he wasn't amused by this witch. "I always warn because the chase is part of the fun."

Once more her laughter rang out. "Better be careful, or I might start liking you."

"Does this mean you'll help?"

Deino crouched to grab her dog and tuck it under her arm. "I'll get back to you about it. I want to talk to Frieda about my future first."

"She might not be able to see it if it requires you to travel to another dimension."

"Perhaps not, but she can tell if I'll come back."

"When will you have an answer?" he asked as she once more dared to walk away.

She cast him a coy glance over her shoulder. "I'll call you."

Should he point out he didn't have a phone? In his day, prayer was enough to get his attention. In his day, she would have never refused.

And even more disrespectfully, she made him wait.

# 3

As I walked away from the monster god, I added an extra wiggle to my step.

"What do you think, Jinx?" I murmured. "Is he staring at my ass?"

My dog glanced behind. "*Yip.*"

He totally was.

I smirked. Vain? Totally. What woman wouldn't want to be admired by a god, even one lacking his gifts? A god who wanted me to help him.

"He wants me to go traipsing in some alternate dimensions. How crazy is that?" I muttered to my pet.

"*Bark.*"

"Yeah, it does sound exciting. And the thought of more power...." Enough to be immortal... I wouldn't deny being tempted. "Think he's the type to double cross?"

*"Grr."*

"No, he doesn't seem like it. But then again, dude's gotta be a little crazy after being locked away by his lonesome for so long."

At least he'd kept fit while in prison. The man looked fine. More than fine. I had to wonder why he'd been hiding his face before. I'd never seen him without the hood. There had been some debate among me and my sisters as to what hid under that robe of his. We'd assumed horrible disfigurement or non-human body parts. Thus far, everything I'd seen looked scrumptious. It didn't hurt I'd always had a thing for gentleman types in suits.

Back at my apartment, I wiped off Jinx's little paws before giving her some treats. "Who's my good girl?" I cooed.

Spin. Spin. *"Bark. Bark."* She then proceeded to run to the shag, squat, and pee.

Goddammit!

I cast a spell of odor repelling and chided my dog. "Bad girl."

Jinx turned the biggest, most apologetic eyes on me.

"It's okay. I know you're a good girl. Who's my baby?" I held out my arms. Jinx came sprinting into them, a wiggly fur ball of love. And to think my sisters called her demon dog.

So maybe she didn't like many people. Actually, no one but me. With me, she could be the most loveable little furball ever! How could I think of leaving Jinx to go hunting after a psycho, power-stealing twat? But what if not dealing with it now caused problems down the road?

I glanced at the clock. Almost four, which made it about ten my sister's time. Still early enough to call.

The connection rang and rang before it went to voicemail, where Frieda said, "I'm busy, Dina. It can wait until the morning. Do not leave a message at the beep."

*Beep.*

"So Typhon paid me a visit and wants me to go dimension hopping, looking for Ariadne. He wants his power back and demands I help him. Have to admit, kind of intrigued. Who knows, maybe I'll find Mom."

My mom, a.k.a. the goddess of betrayal, Apate, a.k.a. the big, fat liar. Turns out my mother played a part in Ariadne stealing from Typhon. The goddess of betrayal answered Ariadne's prayer to betray her husband, Bacchus. Apate gave Ariadne some magical tools to get even with Bacchus, whom she claimed was going to set her aside for a mistress.

Rather than use the magic-controlling collar on her husband, Ariadne ended up snaring Typhon, a much more powerful god. And he wasn't the only one. Ariadne must have found more of the collars and armbands, seeing as how she'd enslaved two other deities for their power.

Obviously not what Apate had planned when she'd answered the prayer.

It took Mom centuries to plot her revenge. It involved giving birth to triplets, and then—via a special ceremony on our sixteenth—bless us in the monster god's name. All stuff we didn't find out until recently.

We had so many questions. However, the answers were lost when Mom got tossed through an interdimensional door. I might have worried more, but Bacchus, Ariadne's very unhappy husband, jumped in after her. Given they used to date, I assumed they'd take care of each other and get back if they could.

Enyo had suggested we go hunting for Mom. I was more than willing to try to open a portal to another world, but Frieda had shaken her head. "Waste of time. Whether you go or not, she'll end up coming back. Eventually."

I remember blinking at my sister. "Since when can you read Mom's future?" It had always been a pet peeve of hers that she couldn't see it.

Frieda had a secretive smile as she'd said, "I can do a lot of things now."

But apparently answering the phone wasn't one of them. Despite leaving a message, and texting, she didn't return my call.

I waited. Watched some television. Magically ran a dusting rag over my shelves then made a wet mop dance on the floor *Fantasia* style. Around six, I made myself dinner. More boob tube, still no call back. At eight o'clock, out of boredom, I went to bed. After all, morning for Frieda happened early my time. She couldn't avoid me forever.

The moment I fell asleep, I dreamed I was back in Ariadne's throne room in the castle she'd built—

or stolen—high atop some mountain. In the seat of her power, we'd confronted her—my mom, me, my sisters, and their boyfriends. Even Typhon showed up, looking like the Grim Reaper with his wisping robe. The fight hadn't been all that great since Ariadne kept using an ability she'd stolen to lock up our magic. Frieda evened the odds by figuring out how to remove the armband giving Ariadne that specific power. At that point, the tide shifted, and the bitch chickened out by jumping into a portal.

After, I'd asked Frieda if we'd ever see Ariadne again, and she'd been evasive. Her reply of, "Depends," was as much as she'd say. Depends on what? Given Typhon's request today, I had a feeling I knew who it depended on and so did Frieda. I hadn't forgotten she'd tried to keep me from running into him.

Thinking of my sister conjured her in my dream. She appeared by the dais, looking pensive.

I shook a finger and chided, "You better not be dream-walking inside my head."

Frieda had gone from being the most fragile of us sisters to wielding some seriously cool powers, such as being able to leave her body and travel the astral plane.

"Afraid I'll see something?" she taunted.

"Do you really want to know what I do with my vibrator?"

"Ew, really, Dina!" Frieda exclaimed.

"Masturbation is healthy," I said with the kind of toothy smile that I knew drove her nuts.

"I wouldn't know since my husband takes care of my needs daily," was her sly rejoinder.

I'll admit my jaw dropped. She never used to have comebacks. "Touché, dear sister. Now, care to tell me why you and I are here in this wretched place?"

"I thought you wanted to talk." Frieda glanced at me, looking more relaxed than I recalled. She'd not only finally figured out how to control her abilities, she'd also fallen in love. It looked good on her.

"I wanted to talk on the phone, not here." I waved a hand.

"I work in the morning, so why not now? This is about Typhon, right?"

"You knew I was going to run into him."

"I told you to stay inside."

"Well, I didn't. He wants me to help him find Ariadne," I told her, despite the fact she most likely already knew.

"And you said no." Stated, not asked.

"I said I'd think about it."

Frieda gaped at me. "What's there to think about?"

"He offered me immortality."

Frieda stared without blinking for a moment. "Okay, I can see why you'd be tempted. But still, we're talking about Ariadne with the power of a god at her fingertips."

"Which we dealt with already. And at the time, she technically had the power of three gods." But Frieda had managed to fry off two of her controlling bands, leaving only Typhon's.

"She won't be taken unaware again."

"You speak as if you know. I thought you couldn't see outside this world?" I accused.

"I only see the parts that happen here."

Which is when it hit me. "You do see some futures where she returns."

"Yes, but I'm working on severing their paths." She waved a hand as she said the kookiest thing.

"I take it it's bad when she returns."

My sister struggled to not reply before sighing. "Yes. But that doesn't mean you need to confront her."

In other words, I did. Frieda would only be

trying this hard if she saw a rough path ahead. One where I died. Not the optimal outcome, but neither was Ariadne returning.

"Do you know where Ariadne is?" I asked.

Freida shook her head. "I haven't seen anything."

"How long before she comes back?"

Freida shrugged. "Nothing I've seen gives me a date."

"What about me? Let's say I were to go looking for her..." I trailed off, and Frieda grimaced.

"If you go with him, you won't come back the same."

"Well, I will be immortal if I win. I'd better make sure I'm looking my best in case I'm stuck in whatever look I'm wearing." Eyebrows, a facial, and a nice haircut. Better hit a few spin classes too.

Frieda shook her head. "I wouldn't want to be immortal. It's a long time."

"Which is exactly the point." The things I could do and discover...

"That will depend on the future you choose," was Frieda's low rebuke.

"Lay it on me. How do I die?" Best start avoiding it now.

"There are some paths where you leave this dimension and I don't see you coming back."

"But you can't be sure I'm dead. I could just be stuck."

Her lips flattened. "In the ones where you do return, you're different."

"Different how? Am I injured? Old?"

"It's difficult to explain."

I rolled my eyes. "Way to make it more dramatic. How about you answer me this... in the futures where I return, is it because I defeated her?"

She offered a single nod but didn't look happy about it.

"That's good news. Why do you seem all bent out of shape?"

"Because you're different. And it's not a good thing." She bit her lower lip before whispering, "You're essentially an evil sorceress who brings about the apocalypse."

Well damn. I stared at her then smiled. "And you're sure of that, or is it just an interpretation? Because let's be honest, given how I like to shop and travel, I would need a damned good reason to end the world."

"The visions haven't been long enough to explain why you do it, only that you're very powerful and angry, so very angry. You're, like, floating, all super mutant in the sky with lightning flashing out from you, and there's destruction all around, but you don't care."

"Maybe next time you get that vision take a look around for some enemies. Could be I go bad-ass superhero taking out a threat. No way am I destroying the world because then there would be no designer purses, no crazy expensive shoes, no fancy restaurants." Just a few of my favorite things.

"This isn't funny, Dina. I am seriously worried."

"You're always worried, French fry." My sister had literally cried wolf so many times in my life and Enyo's that we no longer listened when she screamed catastrophe if we didn't follow her instructions.

"Don't make me kill you for being a psycho evil sorceress intent on destroying the world," she sobbed.

"Wait, have you actually seen that happening?"

"No." She sniffled. "But who else could get

close enough to end your reign of terror?"

I blinked at my sister. "You are fucking with me."

Frieda's tears suddenly dried up. "No. I do see you going nuts, but at the same time, the Ariadne futures aren't any better, which means I'd rather take my chances with you. Maybe you are meting out mega destruction to do good."

"Way to sound convinced," was my dry reply.

"I know you. I've seen you on the rag. Now add god powers? You could be capable of erasing men if one so much as looked at you sideways."

"Would not."

She arched a brow.

I conceded. I would.

"Well, you have a bit of time before you need to worry," I said. "I don't have anything in my wardrobe that I'd be willing to be seen in on social media. The right look is needed, or I could end up with a horrendous villain name."

"It's like you want to be killed," Frieda wailed.

"Love you too, French fry." I hugged my dream-walking sister, and it felt real down to the snot wetting the shoulder of my shirt.

Ew.

She gave it one last wipe before mumbling, "Something's wrong."

"What is it?"

"Wake up. Wake up. NOW!" she yelled.

I sat bolt upright in my bed to hear Jinx growling, probably because everything was shaking!

# 4

An earthquake? I didn't live in a place that had a fault line and, until now, had never felt a single tremor.

I rolled out of bed as everything shook. Given the way the building trembled, I needed to get outside, but I doubted I'd have time to get changed out of my silky tank and shorts. So be it. I usually wore less at the beach.

I snared my dog and grabbed a robe off a hook as I drunkenly walked to the door of my apartment. This quake seemed unnaturally long. Didn't they last mere seconds usually?

Before I could put my hand on the doorknob,

the floor heaved hard enough I lost my balance, hitting my ass and sliding.

*Oomph.* The sudden slam into a wall knocked the breath from me, and my dog yelped.

"Sorry." I tried to shove to my feet, but the unnatural tilt of the building made it impossible. It didn't help that the building still shivered ominously. Things creaked that shouldn't creak. Electrical popped, spitting sparks. Fire seemed unlikely, given water also sprayed from my kitchen, which didn't make the slippery situation any better. Not to mention, being electrocuted didn't sound like much fun.

I had to get out of here. The door I'd been heading for would lead me to the stairs, but did I want to be enclosed in a stairwell if the whole thing collapsed? The window made sense, and before anyone wondered, I didn't have to worry about gravity because, hello, I was a witch.

"Time to float." The magic enveloped me and my dog, lifting us in a bubble. I used that moment to slip on my robe before snaring my dog close. As I headed for the window, my purse— hanging on a hook by the front door—and a pair of shoes floated after us.

With a wave of my hand, the glass in the window shattered before I neared. Another flick of my fingers and all the shards cleared the frame. Before I drifted past it, I exerted even more of my magic, creating an invisibility shield against anyone watching, a difficult thing to maintain while moving. However, given today's prevalence of cameras, better to be safe rather than end up some eternal meme. At least I wore underwear, so if someone did peek up my robe, my bits were covered.

A good thing I'd taken precautions because there was already a crowd. People noticed the leaning structure, and the dumbasses came gawking. Like, did they not see it would fall any moment?

I gritted my teeth as I floated down, hoping my dog wouldn't start barking. She hated being stared at. She behaved, and yet I didn't completely escape notice. A few people thought they saw something by the way they pointed. Their keen interest would make it hard to drop my shield. I needed a distraction. One arrived in the form of the building shuddering and making ominous creaking noises.

People finally decided it might be a good idea to get out from under its shadow. I joined the tail end of the crowd, shoes on my feet, purse over my shoulder, dog tucked under my arm. I snuck behind a big dude before dropping my shield. He'd block anyone filming in this direction.

When my apartment building collapsed, the impact rumbled the ground and a wave of dust exploded. Since I didn't plan to choke to death, I flung up a new barrier as wide as I could to mitigate the worst of it.

There was much coughing, although not by those nearest me. Given I'd cleared the danger zone, I turned to look behind and couldn't help but gape. My home was gone. Only a pile of rubble remained.

All my shoes. Purses. That gorgeous designer dress I'd paid a fortune for. Every single memory I'd collected.

Before I could curse the earthquake that caused the destruction, I noticed movement at the base of my building. Odd since I was the only one home at the time.

I paused to stare at the ruined basement, where a water pipe sprayed into the air, which, in turn, caused the dust to turn heavy and settle. Maybe I'd imagined seeing something.

My dog growled, her little body vibrating in

my grip as a monster, the size of a large dog and the likes of which I'd never seen or heard of clambered over the edge of the gaping hole. Part insect, part who the fuck knew. Might have been an alien. And it didn't come alone.

More of the alien bugs poked conical heads over the ruined concrete basement, their spear-tipped limbs climbing with ease over the destruction. The first one to clear the edge and get me in its view raised a pincer-tipped arm and chittered in my direction.

Yes mine. And, no, I wasn't being vain. My building had just been taken down, and monsters had appeared in the basement. It seemed safe to assume they'd come for me or my sisters.

The alien bug was joined by its friends, and they proceeded to make some god-awful noise as they rubbed their spear-tipped limbs together before charging.

I wasn't the only one who spotted them. No surprise, the invasion of oversized bugs led to people screaming. Loudly. Between that and the crash of my home, I wasn't sure if my ears would ever recover.

As folks ran—and gave me some space—I set my dog down, tightened the sash on my robe, and took in a breath to growl, "You fuckers wiped out decades of fashion collecting. Prepare to die."

As the leader came skittering for me, I pointed my hand and, with very little effort, blasted it to pieces. It exploded in a spray of chunks and yellowish-green ichor. The chunks hit the ground and stopped moving. They didn't reconstitute. Good.

I flung both my hands toward the rest of the bugs.

*Splat. Splat.*

I totally had this. Jinx cheered me on, barking as she ran back and forth by my feet.

The half-dozen bugs that had climbed from my basement and thought they could get me died, and I smiled. A smile that lasted until the ground shook.

I braced myself, and my dog froze at my feet. From the hole, something big began pushing through. A huge conical head, and I mean massive.

My mouth rounded as I breathed, "What the fuck is that?"

"Vermonstra." Typhon suddenly spoke from beside me. "Or in simple terms, monster worm."

I cast him a glare. "You destroyed my home!"

"This isn't my fault," he stated, his gaze intent on the monster still heaving itself from the hole.

"Then whose fault is it a monster took out my home, oh monster god?" I snapped.

"Yours."

"Mine?" I yelled as the sinuous body stopped rising and the head began swaying side to side as if seeking something.

"Yes, yours. Ariadne might be gone from this world, but her influence remains. She's sending her minions after you."

"Me?" I squeaked as the head turned in my direction, eyeless, and yet I knew it saw me.

"You are a threat. Therefore, she wants to eliminate you."

As he spoke, the worm slammed down. Only I had already moved, not needing Typhon's hand on my arm to tug me out of harm's way. Luckily Jinx knew when to scamper and barked from a distance.

While the mega worm was down, I flung magic on it, only to have it shatter against its thick skin.

The body took its time rising and once more wavering in the air as it sought me out again. I noticed as I moved it shifted to keep track of me.

"It has no eyes. How does it know where I am?" I asked.

"Magic. Specifically, anyone with my magic," Typhon said as the worm once more tried to smash me.

I floated myself out of reach before snapping, "That can't be right. You're the original god. You still have some magic. Why isn't it going after you?"

"Because I'm not the one leaking all over the place."

Wait, I was leaking? Gross. "How do I stop it?"

"By not letting it seep."

Because that explained how. I shot him a dirty look a second before I snatched my dog and flung myself sideways, using my magic to float me into a soft landing. The slamming vermonstra head cracked the pavement.

It didn't seem keen on leaving its hole, but would it follow me if I left?

I began to retreat, Jinx tucked against me, my gaze fixed on the worm that rose higher than before. High enough that its next slam brought it within feet of my position.

How much more of the worm was still underground? And if it slithered free, how fast would it be?

I needed to stop this.

"Any suggestions?" I yelled at Typhon.

"You could try killing it."

"How?" I asked. "I tried magic, but it can't penetrate."

"I've heard that being swallowed and exploding it from the inside is effective. But I don't suggest that, given the stomach acid might digest you before you can escape its guts."

"There must be another way."

"I don't suppose you have any explosives?"

I glared at him.

He shrugged. "You asked for ideas."

"How about something that won't get me killed?"

"If you wish for it to leave you alone, shut off your magic so it can't see you."

"Magic doesn't turn off."

"Says someone who's never tried," he scoffed.

Why would I? From the moment I'd found my power, I'd been cultivating it. Practicing it to its limits, pushing to try and get stronger. Now I could do insane things. Blow up giant insects, open portals, throw lightning.

The vermonstra swiveled, passed right over Typhon, and saw me again.

Saw my magic.

Dammit, Typhon spoke the truth. My inability to mask my power was why it kept coming for me. Just like how those monsters used to go for Frieda when she was leaking her magic all the time.

Shut it off. Easier said than done. I'd never tried to cram it into a box. But I did now. Wedged it into a tiny space and felt naked without it. The vermonstra paused, then swiveled left, right. It kept whipping back and forth, seeking and not finding. Well, damn. It worked.

"We should probably relocate," Typhon stated as he neared me while the confused worm kept scenting the air.

"Shouldn't we do something about the monster? There are people in this neighborhood."

"Some of whom appear to be returning with guns," he pointed out, drawing my gaze to a guy dressed in construction oranges with a rifle in hand. "I also hear sirens, which most likely means police and more weapons. Do you really want to be here when everyone starts firing at the vermonstra?"

I winced. The panic would be real.

Suddenly my dog wiggled, and I lost my grip. She hit the ground without stumbling, taking off on her short little legs for a stray bug thing crawling from the hole, which somehow found a space to get past the girth of the vermonstra.

My dog went right for it.

"Baby, no!"

The alien bug spat goo on my dog, putting her to sleep. Or so I hoped. Jinx fell over but still seemed to be breathing.

"You fucker! No one messes with my baby!" I blasted the monster to bits.

Yes, I used magic, and too late remembered the monster above.

A glance showed the vermonstra rigid and again looking right at me.

I could have hidden my magic and dove to the side, but amidst that gooey mayhem, my dog woke. She wavered on groggy legs and uttered little yips.

I flung a fist of magic to grab my pet, even as my other hand shot upwards, hoping I could shove a fist of power into the monster and knock it aside.

It failed, and I saw death come slamming for me.

In that jaw-clenching, heart-stopping moment, I heard a word. Not one I understood, but I felt it reverberating through my body and soul.

A word of power.

The last syllable hung in the air, and the world paused.

I opened my eyes to see the vermonstra had halted its attack. Floating before its massive face, once more in his cloak, was Typhon with his arms outstretched.

"Begone." Typhon spoke normally, and yet the vermonstra obeyed. It retreated back into the hole it dug, but that didn't bring back my precious apartment.

Typhon floated to the ground and staggered.

I grabbed his arm to steady him, feeling the thickness of his biceps through the strange slippery nature of his cloak. "How did you do that? I thought Ariadne took your god monster powers."

"She did. And that attempt by me to use them wasn't a good idea," he muttered before slumping at my feet.

I glanced at him then my dog, who cocked her head at me. "You know, I am tempted to leave him here." But he had answers, and he had just saved me and Jinx from the worm.

"How hard do you think it will be to get him into a hotel room like this?"

Not hard at all, as it turned out. I prepaid the room online, got my virtual key, and floated his ass right onto the bed.

A king-sized bed, but from the way he reacted when he woke up... Well, let's just say it became pretty apparent he'd not slept with anyone in a while.

And I couldn't help but be a brat about it.

# 5
## Typhon

"What are you doing?" Typhon growled at Deino. She lay wrapped around him intimately, and it made him vastly uncomfortable. Mostly because he quite enjoyed it for the first few seconds after he woke. He'd even let his fingers stroke her back for a moment, thinking how nice it was, before reality slapped him.

"Good morning. How are you feeling?" she asked, not moving from her spot cuddled on his chest.

"Confused. Where are we?" Last he recalled, he'd stepped in to save the witch, using a power that once came so easily but now required him to strain with all his might to project. But what choice did he have? The vermonstra would have killed his only hope.

"We're in a hotel. I rented us a room after you passed out."

"You brought me here?" How god-asculating. Another new low to add to the others.

"Well, I thought about leaving you on the ground for the cops, but Jinx changed my mind."

"Your dog told you to save me?" was his dry reply.

Said dog made noise from somewhere in the room.

"Oddly enough, Jinx likes you, and considering that's a first, I decided to be nice. Hence why I deigned to share my room with you."

"And you couldn't find one with two beds?" He knew many rental establishments offered the option.

"It's not a big deal." She snuggled her face deeper against him.

"This is inappropriate."

"Totally," she agreed.

"Then why aren't you moving?"

"Because it's been ages since I've woken up beside a man, and I'm going to enjoy it before you annoy me so much I start thinking of ways to kill you."

He hated how much he enjoyed her sassy retorts. In his day, a woman would have bowed and showered him with nothing but flattery. "If you kill me, then I can't help you with the monsters."

She lifted her head to look him in the face. "Good point. I'll keep you alive for now, I guess, but only if you start giving me some answers."

"Are you always this demanding?"

"Yes."

He eyed her. Almost smiled. Damned if he didn't quite like her. "Will replying to your questions help you to realize why you should aid me?"

"Depends on what you say."

"This seems an awkward position for such a serious discussion."

"You're right. I should be in a more commanding position." As she spoke, she shifted until she straddled him, wearing only a silky top and very short bottoms. His body reminded him it hadn't been with a woman in a long time. Despite how hard he clenched his fists and teeth, he couldn't help but react.

She noticed.

Her lips curved. "So, tell me, am I going to be

dealing with monsters coming after me on a daily basis?"

"Not daily. I imagine it's not easy for Ariadne to send them after you from wherever she is. Not to mention, some will go after your sisters."

She rocked on him as she took on a pensive expression while torturing him. "What will it take to stop these monster attacks? And don't tell me killing Ariadne. I am not doing your dirty work."

"You could rid yourself of my blessing. No magic, no reason for her to come after you."

"Not happening." She waved a hand, dismissing the suggestion, as he'd expected. "What else?"

"Keep it tucked away at all times."

"Easier said than done, and that doesn't help my sisters. I don't know if Enyo can put her strength in a tiny mental box."

"Then I guess you'll be killing lots of monsters."

"Yeah, no. Bad enough one destroyed my home."

"You know the only permanent solution is to remove my power from Ariadne. As their god, I would keep the monsters in line." He shrugged, including a thrust of his hips. Her breath caught, and definite heat seeped through her thin garments.

She pressed her palms into his chest and leaned down so that her hair formed a curtain around her face. "Let's say I agreed to help. How would we even find her?"

He couldn't help but put his hands on her hips, even as he restrained an urge to grind himself against Deino. "There is a place I know that might be able to divine her location."

"Where?"

"It's in another dimension, but you'd have to come with me."

"Why not go yourself?"

"Because I don't have the magic to open the doorway needed to get there." An embarrassing truth.

"Is the monster god admitting he needs me?" she purred, leaning down low, putting pressure on him.

His fingers dug into her flesh. "Yes." In more ways than he cared to admit.

"Say please."

"You would make me beg?"

Her lips curved, and her hips rocked ever so slightly. "Tell me you need me."

"I need you." He couldn't stop himself from saying it.

"What's the magic word?"

He groaned as she kept up the subtle pressure. Her nails dug into his chest as she gyrated her hips on him, causing him to catch his breath and for his own fingers to hold her hips tight. They said nothing, but her forehead pressed to his as their bodies rolled and rubbed, separated by fabric and yet it didn't matter. When she shuddered and uttered a small gasp of pleasure, he clenched hard so as to not embarrass himself.

Her eyes opened, and she moistened her lips before she offered a husky, "I need to freshen up. Then I'll shop for some stuff."

"What stuff?" He felt slightly stupid and tense. What had just happened?

"If we're going on a trip, then I need clothes." She slid off him and stood beside the bed. "These are quite dirty." With that, she shimmied out of said clothes and stalked naked to the bathroom.

He could only stare, in that moment more mortal than he'd ever been. His balls were tight and aching from the aborted climax. He'd almost spilled when she'd been grinding against him. Had wanted nothing more than to flip her onto her back before laying claim to those lips—and that body.

Yet, he'd abstained. He'd not meant to get entangled with the witch. He needed her to help him with Ariadne. Nothing more. Anything else was just a distraction.

Typhon rolled off the bed, his cloak billowing around him, the one thing Ariadne hadn't taken. He smoothed his hand down the front, and it changed to something more suitable for the time. A suit, as he didn't like the casual wear he'd been seeing.

He could hear water running as Deino took a shower. Her naked body was being sluiced by water. Her hands soaping her smooth flesh. Stroking between her legs.

He whirled from staring at the door and glared at his cock instead. Since when did it misbehave? Sure, it had been a while since he'd been with a woman, but he'd long passed the age where he didn't control his erections.

Now would be a good time to remind himself that Deino toyed with him and that he couldn't afford to do anything that would jeopardize his main quest: Getting his power back.

For that he needed Deino working with him,

not mad because they became lovers and had a quarrel.

But she made it hard.

Literally, hard.

"*Yip.*"

He eyed the dog standing at his feet. "What?"

The dog whirled to look at the door to the room. He swung his head to look. The handle rattled.

He put his finger to his lips, and the dog nodded before flanking the door.

The lock clicked, and the portal swung open.

Jinx went ballistic, barking.

Not that Enyo seemed to care. She walked in, eyed him, and then the room. "Where's my sister?"

"Bathroom."

Enyo didn't knock, just went inside, releasing a cloud of steam before the door shut.

While Jinx caught her breath, Bane entered the hotel room, and the dog truly went mental, barks shrill enough even Typhon winced. He scooped up the mutt, and it instantly quieted.

Bane sighed. "Damn, that thing is loud." He closed the door to the room.

Typhon eyed the man who'd been one in a

line of many who'd been tasked with keeping him locked away. He harbored no hatred. The Wardens might have kept him prisoner, but they'd been misinformed as to why.

The former Warden eyed him with curiosity, and it was then it occurred that Bane had no idea who Typhon was. After all, in previous encounters, Typhon had been wearing a hood.

So it was with surprise he heard Bane drawl, "I told Enyo you had a face."

"How did you know?"

"Smell never lies." Bane tapped his nose.

"I assume Enyo's abrupt arrival is because of the incident." Had Deino contacted her? She'd not mentioned it. Then again, he'd not asked if she'd talked to anyone. He'd been distracted.

"Way to downplay." Bane snorted. "Seems like more than a little incident. The building got knocked over by some giant, underground worm. It's all over social media. The number of videos from all kinds of angles is nuts, including a few that Deino needs to know about." He jerked his head in the direction of the bathroom. "And you made it into a few as well. Some you're wearing a suit, others your robe."

Unfortunate. "Is Deino in danger?" In his time, some cultures would have punished a witch.

"Not from humans—not yet—but her actions are causing some questions. Luckily, most people assume it's some kind of deepfake, but there are others who might dig deeper. She should be fine if she lies low for a while," Bane stated before asking, "What happened? Seems like that worm and those monsters really wanted a go at her."

"It would seem Ariadne is still managing to cause trouble despite her relocation."

"She put a hit out on Dina?"

"She most likely is pushing those still listening to her to attack all three of the sisters," Typhon corrected.

"Which explains the problems we've been having since we split up after Ariadne's disappearance."

"Enyo's been attacked?" Typhon hadn't been aware.

"Yeah, but she assumed it was just monsters being monsters." Bane rubbed his jaw. "I take it this will keep happening until we handle Ariadne."

"It seems likely."

"Okay. So when do we leave to hunt down her ass?"

"We?"

"Enyo and I will help of course."

The offer surprised him. "You will? But I haven't even asked." He'd gone after the toughest one to convince and the one he most needed because of the magic she wielded.

"Yeah, according to Frieda's visions, you would have requested our aid but at a later date. Rather than dance around the bush, we chose to come preemptively to offer our services."

Before Typhon could reply, the bathroom door opened, and a towel-swaddled Deino emerged with her sister to announce, "They're coming with us."

"So I've been told," was Typhon's dry reply.

"Frieda and John will be here soon as they can catch a flight. While we wait for them, we can put together a plan and gather some supplies for the trip."

He stared at them in disbelief. "So quickly?"

Deino's lips curved. "What's wrong? Don't like it fast?" She winked. "You should know by now the Grae sisters don't mess around."

"It will be dangerous." He couldn't have said

why he felt a need to mention that. He wanted this to happen, so why try and convince them otherwise?

Enyo arched a brow. "You don't need to sell it to me. I'm already in."

It led to Typhon frowning at Deino. "What happened to not involving your family?"

"Testing you. You passed, by the way. Besides, alone we're deadly, together we're..." She offered a tight predator smile. "Unstoppable."

An ominous prediction.

# 6

Good thing my sister hadn't barged in on me two seconds earlier in the shower while I relived the embarrassingly good orgasm I'd had from grinding against Ty. A grown-ass woman shouldn't get off dry humping, and yet I'd leaned against that shower wall, my legs wobbly, because damn. Who knew an interrogation could be so intense?

Then Enyo, with no boundaries whatsoever, interrupted my shower.

"Dina! What the fuck? You okay? Why didn't you call? I am going to fuck up that worm!"

I popped my head around the curtain to see

Enyo standing in the steamy bathroom. "I'm fine. How the fuck did you find me?"

Enyo rolled her eyes. "Please. If you wanted to hide, don't use your credit card."

Point taken. "I assume you heard what happened to the apartment building."

"Don't you mean saw? It's all over the internet. Videos of our place falling over and then some bug people attacking, followed by a giant fucking worm trying to turn you into pink paste."

I winced. "Fuck me, I was worried about that."

"Duuuude." She drew out the word. "There's a shit-ton of videos, and some are bad. Like the ones of you pointing your fingers and splatting the bugs. And then there was Reaper"—the name we used to call Typhon when we didn't know his identity—"floating in the sky, giving the worm the stink eye. The amount of speculation going on now is insane. Some people are saying it was a stunt for a movie."

"Pretty elaborate stunt," I muttered, turning off the shower and grabbing a towel.

"The theories are crazy. I even heard someone tied it to climate change, saying it's affecting the earth's core and waking up things that have long been sleeping."

At that, I snorted. "For fuck's sake. Not everything has to do with the latest social media frenzy." I had to wonder what would come after the climate thing died down.

"Anyhow, you might want to lie low for a bit because chances are the wrong people saw what happened."

"The government can't hold me." I'd played with handcuffs and various cells just to make sure.

"Not talking about the feds. The Arcane League isn't happy, according to John." John being my sister Frieda's new husband and the League being the magical police.

"How can I be in trouble? The worm and those giant bugs came after me. I was simply defending myself."

"With magic. In public. Big no-no," she reminded me unnecessarily.

I rolled my eyes. "Too fucking bad. I wasn't dying to preserve the arcane secret. We all know it's only a matter of time before it all blows up anyhow."

"I think that time is now. I swear, since Ariadne left, the news has had daily reports of unexplained phenomena. It's like without someone to keep them in line, the monsters are coming out of the woods, bogs, and ground. It's going to be great for business." Enyo grinned. My mercenary sister loved a good fight.

"Does Frieda know to watch for monsters?" I used to worry a lot about her wellbeing when she was a recluse. Now, she might be the scariest of us three.

For some reason Enyo found that exceedingly funny given her laughter. "I swear they're scared of her."

They should be. My sister had found a way to sever living things from having a future. Instant death. I was only a little jealous. My methods tended to be messier.

Speaking of messy... "You don't think Bane killed my dog, do you?" Because Jinx had gone from psychotic to quiet. Usually only I could calm her.

"He might have if he got hungry." Enyo shrugged.

My baby!

With a towel tucked around my boobs, I emerged from the bathroom, ready to freak, only to find my dog in the monster god's arms, looking quite content. A surprise. No one was usually allowed to touch her other than me.

Which led to me covering my sudden exit by announcing my sister would be joining us on our quest.

"So I hear," Typhon murmured without meeting my gaze.

Hmm. Was someone feeling shy after our little interlude? He shouldn't. I planned to maul him again, more thoroughly next time.

Given the room had too many people standing around, I took charge. "We'll need travel packs, given we can't be sure what to expect where we're going. Clothing, medical supplies, food. We should include some form of currency." I glanced at Typhon. "Gold, silver? What works best?"

"Depends on the dimension. Although I should mention any items unique to this world would be accepted when bargaining."

"So knickknacks, snacks, books?"

At his nod, Enyo declared, "On it. Bane and I will also load up on weapons and ammo just in case we end up in a situation where magic doesn't work."

"Be sure to load up on grenades," I suggested, remembering the worm. "Oh, and don't forget knives, too, in case it's like the cavern where combustion didn't work." A reminder that we'd come across a place once before where guns wouldn't fire.

As the pair left, I eyed Typhon, who chose to ignore me in favor of petting my dog. Unacceptable. I dropped my towel and walked toward the phone on the nightstand, intentionally crossing his line of sight.

"Do you need me to order you a wardrobe?" I asked coyly over my bare shoulder.

To those wondering, yes, he stared. He also had a fantastic hard-on.

"I'm fine," he managed to mutter through gritted teeth.

"You sure? You don't look fine."

"The dog needs air. We're going outside," he barked before he fled the room.

I couldn't help but smirk. Nice to know I could affect a god.

While he escaped and tried to get his erection under control, I called the front desk and ordered room service. Then it was to my cell phone where a few special orders were placed. A good thing I knew some shops. Within the hour, deliveries began to arrive.

Shoes. Boots. Pants. Undergarments. I soon had a variety spread out. I chose to wear a comfortable jumpsuit with cute runners as I folded and packed the rest, my new satchel quickly bulging, leading to me pouting when Typhon returned with Jinx, who chose to nap in the remaining heap.

"That's much too unwieldy," he pointed out as he eyed the straining seams of my bag.

"I didn't know what kind of weather to pack for, so I had to cover a little of everything. Not all of us can use magic to make suits, you know." I cast him a glance from under my lashes.

"It's the cloak. It can change into whatever I picture."

"So the cloak is magic?" For some reason, this amused me. "How did you make it?"

"It was a gift."

"Useful gift." I leaned back from the satchel that still didn't have half the clothes I wanted, not to mention not a single hair care or skin care product yet. I sighed. "I miss my old bag with its added dimensional pocket."

"Why not create a new one?"

"Because they're not easy to make," I countered. If they were, I wouldn't have turned my spare bedroom into another closet. A closet now lost. Sob. "I bought the last one I had."

"Have you even tried to create your own?" he countered.

"No, because I don't know where to start."

"I can guide you in its creation," he offered.

"Is this where you take over my body like you did to Frieda? Because I'm telling you right now, I won't be your puppet."

"Your sister was too panicked the times she asked for my aid, so it was the most expedient solution. You are not being attacked, nor are you terrified. I'd say you can handle instruction."

"Lucky me, the monster god as my teacher," I mocked, and yet I dumped out my bag and held it out. "What do we do first?"

"First you must secure some empty space."

I blinked. "Um, say that again."

He clasped my hands. "It sounds odd, and yet that is the simplest explanation. You need to claim some empty space and anchor it to the bag."

"And where do I find empty space? Pretty sure I can't buy any at the store. And if you say between my ears, you will regret it."

He frowned. "Between your ears is your brain."

"Good answer. Continue. How do we find what we need?"

"It used to be easier before the Earth became so populated, but there's still much to borrow. For example, the sky overhead, mostly empty and useless."

"Not for airplanes and birds."

"Which is why you grab it from high."

"Grab it how? I can't exactly reach out and close my fingers around it." I kept asking questions because I wanted to understand how the magic worked. In reading spell books and diaries left behind by witches and wizards, I'd discovered that magic was less about words and hand waving and more about shaping intent. Some of the greatest, like Merlin, had taken simple magical concepts and managed to shape their will into incredible things. For example, Merlin's decision to encase a sword in stone that could only be pulled by a noble heart. Of course, Merlin had access to vast stores of power.

"Have you ever travelled without your body?" Typhon asked me.

I thought of my dream with Frieda. "Not intentionally."

"It's not difficult. Even though I'm weak, I can still do it."

"What does astral travel have to do with claiming empty space?"

"Because that's how we'll reach it. Sit with me and relax." He sat midair, legs crossed, as if floating were the normal, relaxing thing to do.

"Won't using magic call monsters?"

"Yes, so let's hope there aren't many around and do this quickly."

I glanced at my dog, who'd been rather well-behaved considering the commotion. "Keep watch on my body."

*"Yip."*

With Jinx on guard, I closed my eyes and joined Typhon in a seated float. It felt weird.

"Relax," he ordered.

"Hard to relax when you want me to leave my body," I grumbled.

"It's a good skill to have."

"Is that how you kept bugging Frieda?"

"It's an excellent way to communicate and spy without risking the physical body," was his smug reply.

"As if you're worried. Gods can't be killed."

"Can't be killed easily," he corrected. "And we can still be hurt. Now, shh. Concentrate."

"Concentrate on what?" I sassed with my eyes shut tight.

"My hand holding yours."

"Is this the start to some weird sex game? Because, just so you know, it doesn't have to be weird. I'm open to trying stuff."

He coughed. "This isn't about intercourse. Now pay attention."

I felt him grab my hand, but when I'd have looked, he murmured, "No peeking yet. Just relax."

His firm grip, cool and tingly, tugged me until I stood, still floating. He kept his hands wrapped around mine as he crooned, "Stepping outside the body isn't hard. It's not getting lost returning to it that's more difficult."

"How can you lose your own body?"

"We can go over the dangers another day. Today, you are learning how to float to find space. Open your eyes."

I opened them to see him in front of me. Outside. In the sky.

Like really, really high.

Gulp.

I'll admit I had a moment of panic. I dare anyone to not feel their stomach plummet if they happened to realize they were floating without a safety net or parachute. Just me and a god.

"How? I didn't even feel my spirit leaving my body."

"Because I might have given you a nudge," he admitted. "You were rather tense."

My lips pursed. "Excuse me for being a little freaked." I still was. I did my best to not gape when I looked down and saw the hotel roof shrinking as we rose.

And kept rising.

It took effort to tamp down my panic, but I wouldn't let it show, not when he looked so bloody calm. "I take it we can't actually fall? Like gravity isn't suddenly going to grab me and smash me into the ground?"

"We are in spirit form and, thus, not subject to physical laws."

"What about my body? How am I supposed to find it?" The hotel was large, and I had to wonder what would happen if my disembodied ass started floating through rooms, looking for it.

"Just follow the tendril tethering you to your body."

A glance showed a silver thread exiting me and stretching downward. His was gold.

"Do I need to worry about something cutting that anchor?" Because it seemed awfully tenuous.

"Hopefully not. But at the same time, we will be using magic, thus making ourselves a target so let's hurry and get what we came for."

We kept floating upward, past the level birds flew at. Then higher than the thin clouds, so thin I didn't see them until we passed through them.

"How far do we have to go?"

"In order to prevent dead zones that humans might notice we should rise above where your planes dare fly. Back in my time, we didn't need to go so far."

"What happens in a dead zone?" I asked, fascinated despite my trepidation.

"Things don't work as they should. Magic. Technology. Time. Things sometimes disappear only to reappear later but changed."

"Reminds me of the Bermuda Triangle." At his blank expression, I explained. "There's a place on the ocean where boats disappear and strange things happen."

"And no one has fixed it?"

"Didn't know it could be fixed."

"A lesson for another day. We're high enough. How much space do you need to pack your things?"

"I don't know. My last satchel had a storage area that was about three feet in diameter."

"That seems small. I'd go larger."

Larger? My greedy heart just about burst in glee. "How do we decide?"

"By cutting out a piece." He held my hand and had me point it outward. "Imagine marking off a section."

Doing our weird floating thing, we traced a huge space, room-sized really, and while I knew my hand couldn't slice, I'd have sworn I saw a line appear in the sky.

"Now we take this section back to the room and your satchel," he advised.

I don't know how I gripped nothing, and yet I dragged space back with me as we suddenly sank a lot faster than we rose. We headed for the hotel in a plummeting way that had me closing my eyes. Which led to him chuckling.

I slammed back into my body, gasping and losing my floating balance. I hit the floor and might have panicked I lost the space we cut out, but Typhon was there, holding nothing, and yet I could tell he still had it.

He nodded at me. "Open the satchel and prepare to attach it to the inside."

"Prepare it how?" I muttered as I yanked it wide open.

"Think of it as stuffing it inside then sewing the edges to your bag."

I don't know how I knew where to push and shove it so that the space ended up inside my oversized purse, but I did. Then following his example, I used my finger to pretend stitch it in place. It seemed too easy. Especially considering what the wizard charged me for my last one.

By the time we were done, my satchel had an entire room's worth of space to toss my shit in, meaning everything I'd bought plus some. With the room emptied of stuff and more on its way, I beamed at Typhon. "It worked."

"As if there was any doubt."

His nonchalant arrogance didn't annoy, but I did wonder if I could take it down a notch. Hence why I grabbed him by the cheeks and planted a kiss on his lips.

He froze.

I leaned away and said, "Thank you."

He might have said something in reply or kissed me back, only a knock at the door startled.

"It's probably my snack," I stated as I opened the door without looking and almost got disemboweled.

# 7

# Typhon

Deino reeled from the doorway, narrowly avoiding a swipe.

"I'm fine," she muttered. "Just stupid."

A lie. Typhon could see a thin tear in her shirt and smell the blood. The attacker had sliced her, and he inwardly seethed.

A creature, covered head to toe in a chitinous armor of dull gray, stepped into the room. It made no sound as it stalked toward Deino, completely ignoring Typhon.

A monster taking no notice of the monster god.

Typhon stepped in front and growled. "Leave her alone."

The thing fixed its red eyes on him, and he had to wonder where it came from, as he'd never encountered the likes of it before.

It went to step around him, and Typhon shifted to block it. "Who sent you?" He pushed some power into the command and forced it to speak.

"Give. Wo. Man." The thing clicked its demand.

"I don't think so," the offended witch snapped. Magic blasted over Typhon's shoulder and hit the intruder, the lightning spreading over its exoskeleton before dissipating.

"Its armor is made to repel magical attacks," Typhon stated before she tried again.

"That's annoying," she complained.

"It means someone sent him on purpose, knowing you couldn't fight it," he said as he used a chair to fend off the creature trying to get around him to grab Deino. "I don't suppose you packed a sword in your satchel."

"Not yet. Enyo was supposed to pick one up."

He ducked as the creature swung its arms. The hands lacked fingers but ended in razor-sharp blades that sheared through the legs of the chair.

As he threw the remains of the chair at the

creature, he shifted his outfit from suit to something more combat-appropriate, meaning heavy with hard boots. Before the creature could swing again, Typhon kicked. The sole connected, and the creature grunted but barely budged. Typhon really wished at times like these that his cloak had a weapons feature.

"How do we kill it?" she asked as the creature swung its knife-tipped hands and missed again.

"Most efficient way? Decapitation."

"Hence why you wanted a sword," she muttered, handing him a lamp.

He ducked under an attack and smashed the object against the creature's skull. It had no effect. The creature shook its head and kept coming, forcing them to retreat to the far wall.

"Can it fly?" she asked, eyeing the window.

"No, but if you're thinking of using magic to toss him, think again."

"That's annoying," she grumbled, hiding behind him. Meanwhile, he was down to using the television he grabbed in passing to block the swinging blows.

"Blame Ariadne. If I had my power, this wouldn't be an issue." Because the monster would be under his command. Didn't matter he'd never encountered it before. The god of them would control.

"Can't you use that fancy word again?" she asked.

"I'm not yet recovered enough from the last time." He hated to admit it.

"Can I use it?"

"Depends. Would you like to still have a mind afterward?"

The monster knew it had them cornered and stomped in for the finish.

"Cover your eyes," Typhon advised as he rushed it, ducking under its swing. He rose up with an arm between its legs, heaving upward, his body weaker than he liked, but still stronger than it used to be when he had his full magic. During his exile, he'd had to learn how to rely on his own wit and muscle.

He heaved, and the armored creature broke through the window to fall to the ground below. A glance showed it shattered enough to no longer be a problem.

Deino blinked at him. "Nice wrestling move."

He wanted to puff his chest at the praise but instead ordered, "Prepare to leave."

"Why?"

"Most likely he was an advance scout."

"Wait, there's more coming?"

"Can we talk about this on the way out of here?"

"My bag is packed." She snared the satchel. Her dog, who'd been surprisingly quiet during the attack, emerged from under the bed, tail wagging.

"Ready?"

"What about Enyo and Bane?" she asked.

"We can call them with our new location. Keep your magic tight."

The moment he opened the door, the mongrel ran out into the hall, barking at the armored invaders emerging from the stairwell. More ominously, the building began to shudder.

"Not the worm again," she muttered. "This is getting ridiculous."

"I didn't expect them to react this quickly to our use of magic." He'd expected a reprieve after the last failed attack.

"Is there anywhere we can go that they can't track me by magic?"

"No."

"Then maybe it's time we left this world."

"Agreed." As he spoke, the elevator opened,

and out spilled Enyo and Bane, loaded with two oversized bags, but more astonishing...

"French fry? I didn't expect you until tomorrow," Deino exclaimed as if they didn't have a horde of marching menace coming for them.

"It *is* my tomorrow." Frieda rolled her eyes.

"Time zone, dude. And to think she's supposed to be the smart one." Enyo snorted. "Now, move out of the way. Monsters to fight." Enyo dropped a heavy bag at their feet as she passed. Bane shed his load as well but waited with them.

"Aren't you going to help her?" asked Deino.

"Bah, in this narrow hall, I'd just get in her way," he scoffed.

Indeed, Enyo needed no help. She pulled a sword she'd sheathed down her back and stood in the middle of the hall. "Come on, you ugly bastards. Pick on my sister, will you?" She rushed them, screaming, and no surprise, with that and the fact the dog continued to bark, someone chose that unfortunate moment to stick their head out of a hotel room door and lost it.

The armored creatures didn't pay any attention to the woman screaming about her headless husband as they aimed for Enyo, who glowed with her particular brand of magic.

Dexterity. Strength. Speed. And she used them all as she battled.

Apate truly had given Typhon some gifted champions. Enyo's blade, an extension of her that flowed and cut and killed. Frieda, meanwhile, whispered with Deino, who nodded and said, "I think I can picture that. Hold on. Let's see if I've got enough juice to get a doorway going."

As the fight raged, the building continued to shudder. Given everyone had a task but him, Typhon did the one thing he knew Deino would appreciate. He grabbed her dog, who gave him a look. "Yes, I know you don't want to be left behind."

Enyo took care of the monsters and returned to them barely winded. "I think that's all of them."

"For now. Time we blew this joint." Deino finished her casting with a flourish, and as a portal opened, a cold breeze fluttered past. A glance within showed nothing but darkness.

He might have asked where it went, only the seer said to her sister, "You visualized the place I showed you."

Deino nodded.

"Dare I inquire where we're going?" the god

of monsters asked, unused to being the last to know.

"To a waypoint that will take us where we need to be," was Frieda's cryptic answer. She winked. "Bundle up, Reaper. It'll be chilly, but we won't be there long."

The party stepped through, Enyo going first with Bane, then Frieda and John with Deino's satchel.

Typhon glanced at Deino, who had a look of concentration as she held open the doorway. While he had the dog tucked under one arm, his other remained free, and for some reason, he clasped her hand before murmuring, "Ready?"

"Do I have a choice?" was her wry reply.

No. But he didn't say it.

They stepped into the portal and emerged in a cavern of ice and rock. A deep chill permeated the place but not for long. John quickly cocooned them in a bubble of warmth as they glanced around.

"What is this place?" Enyo asked.

Frieda repeated, "Access point to other worlds. Or it used to be. Most of the doorways are broken now."

She gestured to the arches carved in stone peppering the space. Of the five they could see, three of them were barely visible for the ice sheeted over them. Another appeared scorched. Leaving only one intact arch. The sigil above was one he recognized and probably not so coincidentally exactly where he'd planned to go.

Enyo stalked in front of the intact arch and squinted at it. "Where's this one go?"

It was Frieda who replied with a cryptic, "This goes where we are supposed to be."

"Way to not answer," grumbled Enyo. "How's it work?"

"You'll see," was the sassy reply by the once fragile sister. She'd grown in confidence since Typhon first met her. Found her courage too. "Follow me."

When Frieda would have stepped through first, her foot passing through the stone in the arch as if it weren't there, Enyo bumped her aside then proceeded to go ahead, Bane at her heels. They walked through seemingly solid stone, the magical passageway not something Typhon could explain. They'd existed long before him. All worlds had at least one, although some had been broken and others required special circumstances, like the eclipse that kept the doorway to his prison world shut.

John held Frieda's hand as they stepped through next, and the warm bubble encasing them disappeared.

Deino shivered. "That is some complex magic. Are we sure it's safe?" She grimaced. "Guess I should have asked before my dumbass sisters decided to go first."

"The place it leads to is known for its neutrality."

"You've used this door before."

"A long time ago."

"Guess we'd better get going before my sisters get in trouble."

Typhon glanced at Deino. "I take it this means you've accepted the bargain I offered."

Her grin tightened his chest. "Let's go kill that twat Ariadne and make me immortal."

# 8

My first thought upon setting foot in a new dimension: We must have used the wrong door because we stepped into a place that looked just like Earth. If I had to name the location, I'd have said Nevada given the hard-baked soil, rocks, and tufts of dry brush and grass. In the distance, I could see the lights of a town. However, I was pretty sure the desert-like state didn't have stone arches with a solid center standing in the middle of nowhere.

I extended my hand, and it went through the rock as if it weren't there. At least the portal seemed to work two ways. Kind of reassuring. If something happened to me, at least my siblings could get home.

My initial impression of the place being like home fell apart at the sight of the fist-sized, bright green glowing thing that went scuttling away from my feet. Jinx wiggled free from Typhon's arms and went chasing with excitement, only to turn tail and yip when the thing flipped around and hissed. My dog went flying into my arms, where I hugged her tight. Meanwhile, the critter farted visible poufs of pink before taking off with dragonfly-type wings.

Definitely not in Nevada.

Overhead hung a cluster of five moons, two of them much brighter than the others, hence why we could still somewhat see. And stars—so many stars—but not all of them twinkling white. I saw red, blue, even purple.

"Where are we?" I breathed.

"Ask Frieda. She's the one who led us here," Enyo stated, slinging her bag to the ground so she could scrounge inside and load herself up with weapons. An impressive amount, I should add, from the sword that got shoved in a sheath down her spine, to side holsters with pistols, and armbands with throwing knives. Another larger-bladed weapon went inside her boot. My sister came to do war.

As for Bane? He stripped, and I turned away quickly before I saw his naked bits. Enyo tended to get a little angry when she caught us looking. In our defense, the man had an incredible physique. Not that I'd admit I noticed if she asked.

"This is where we need to be," Frieda replied. Enough validation for me given the circumstances.

Typhon glanced at Frieda. "How did you know to come here?"

"I saw it."

The simplest answer she could give, yet Typhon frowned. "I didn't know your gift would extend past Earth."

"Me neither." She shrugged. "It hit me suddenly in that hallway. We had two choices in that moment: Get massacred when the building collapsed with us in it because we couldn't get away from those guys in the armor, or continue our quest by coming here."

"What is here?" I asked Typhon. "Do you know this place?"

"Yes. It's called Zuzamenn, a pocket world

created a long time ago as a nexus point for travelers between dimensions," Typhon explained.

"So a crossroads of sorts?" I summarized. "Doesn't seem too welcoming. Where's the signs pointing where to go next?"

Typhon snorted. "Those who come here already know which arch they want next. Those that aren't looking for a new world settle in the town."

"Is Ariadne here?" Enyo asked, frowning at her bag, which still contained a lot of stuff.

As Typhon shook his head, I knelt with my satchel and opened it wide. We stuffed the rest of Enyo's bag, as well as Bane's, within. As a leopard, he couldn't carry anything, and I wanted Enyo's hands free to protect us. John had a knapsack on his shoulder that he held on to, while Frieda had a purse slung cross-body.

"So from here we can go anywhere?" I questioned as I stood up with my still very light satchel.

"Not entirely. Some dimensions are tricky to reach. My former prison, for example, only aligns with Earth under specific conditions." Typhon grimaced. "Ariadne knew what she condemned me to when she trapped me there." With that said, he stared off into the distance.

"How are we supposed to find her? You said someone might be able to help," I reminded.

He shook himself before he replied. "We must bargain with the oracle."

"A seer?" Frieda perked right up.

"She does more than see the future and past. She creates prophecy. Can decide fates. She can be finicky with her aid. If she doesn't like you, or thinks you lack respect, you could find yourself in a great deal of trouble," Typhon cautioned.

"In other words, don't get on her bad side. Got it," Enyo stated. "I'm going to scout around with Spot. Holler if you need me to kill something." She disappeared, a trick she had that allowed her to blend with shadows. Her feline lover went with her.

John eyed Frieda. "How's your wall doing?" He spoke of the mental one Frieda had learned to build to cushion her mind from the millions of possibilities she encountered.

"It's holding steady," Frieda murmured. "But this place is weird. Even with my walls up, I keep seeing phantoms of the past. This spot we're standing on used to be a village, and the whole area used to be a lush forest."

"What happened to it?" I asked, rubbing my face in Jinx's soft fur. It probably hadn't been the best idea to bring her, yet what choice did I have?

Frieda glanced at the sky as she murmured, "Space invaders."

I almost mocked her proclamation, but given how disturbed she appeared, I bit my tongue. "What of the future?" I asked instead. "See any trouble?"

"There are blank spots when I try to look." Her forehead wrinkled. "It's the strangest thing."

John patted her arm. "I get the impression this place messes with magic. Don't force it."

I glanced at Typhon. "Where is this oracle? Cave at the top of a mountain? Guarded by a three-headed dragon?"

"In the town you can see up ahead. She has a small flat above a bread shop."

"Wait, I thought you said she was uber powerful. How is it she doesn't have her own house or a palace?" I questioned, because personally, if I had a cool title like oracle, I'd be sitting on a giant cushion being hand-fed fruit and other yummy stuff.

"She eschews wealth and other accoutrements," Typhon explained as we began to walk.

"Then what are we supposed to bargain with?"

"That will depend on who she's dealing with. Some get away with simple chores such as cooking her a meal or tidying her space. Others have to go on quests and fetch dangerous items. She might even ask for a favor at a later date."

That twisted my lips. "I don't like vague promises of future aid, and I suck at dusting."

"I doubt we'll be given a menial task for what we demand," Typhon murmured as Frieda strolled ahead, arm in arm with John.

"Should I worry?"

"There wouldn't be any point. She will demand. We will have to decide if the price is worth it."

"And if it's too much?"

"Then we will have to find Ariadne another way."

I cast a glance at him. "Not going to try and force us to give the oracle whatever she wants?"

"You are my champions, not my slaves."

"Why, Reaper, I never took you for a benevolent god."

"I'm not. But I'm also not stupid. I can hardly expect you to willingly serve me if I mistreat you. Although call me Reaper again and I might change my mind," he said with a glower.

My laughter echoed louder than I liked in this place. The very quietness of it had me wondering. "Do I have to worry about our magic attracting monsters here?"

"Nothing too dangerous. The true threats have long been extinct. However, in the town, we will likely encounter some beings that might find themselves drawn to you and your sisters."

"Meaning, hold tight to the magic."

"Yes. And whatever you do, don't react first. The guardians of this place respond harshly to violence."

"So let them take the first shot. Got it. Anything else I should know?"

He pursed his lips before sighing. "You may want to inform any who ask that you are claimed."

"Excuse me?"

"Females of power are highly sought by some of the cultures we might encounter. There are many who will see you as a prize worth taking if it is assumed you are not claimed by a male or accompanied by your father or brother."

I couldn't help a snort. "I can't believe I'm hearing this. Misogyny, alive and well in alien places."

"Not all. But some, yes. Females, as the carriers of life, are the most likely of a breeding pair to impart power."

"So is this your way of telling me we have to act like boyfriend and girlfriend while in town?"

He made a face. "That is a repugnant way of describing an intimate relationship."

"So sorry. Would you prefer I call you daddy?" I batted my lashes, and his jaw got that tense look to it again.

"It would be too easy to disprove our lack of shared blood. You will refer to me as your mate."

Again, I couldn't help but laugh. "Mate. Makes us sound like animals."

"All living things are animals. To the fae, we hold less value than their steeds."

"You know, I realize this is a quest to get back your power and get the monsters to ignore me and my sisters, but this is fascinating. I mean my studies of the arcane never led me to realize the vast worlds that existed outside of Earth. Heck, I never expected to encounter things that were considered myth."

"Where do you think legends come from?"

"I would have said imagination."

"How can you imagine something that doesn't exist?" he countered.

"Interesting question." I kicked at the hard ground. "So, this mating thing... Exactly how am I supposed to sell it? Will just saying it be enough, or should I be expecting some PDA?"

"What is PDA?" he repeated.

"Public displays of affection," I explained while grabbing his hand and lacing my fingers with his. "Touching each other in a way that only couples do. Kissing. Intimate smiles and looks that exclude others."

His fingers tightened around mine. "Not necessary, but those would make it convincing. We will also be sharing quarters should we spend the night."

"Awesome. You make a great body pillow."

He growled.

I smiled. "What's wrong? Afraid I'll interrogate you again?"

To my surprise, he stopped dead and spun me

to face him. "You play a dangerous game with your teasing, witch."

"Dangerous how?" I queried, stepping close and tilting my chin. Despite appearing once more like a gentleman, he towered over me.

"You don't want to know."

"And if I did?" I whispered, floating myself upward so our faces aligned.

I don't know what he would have replied because Enyo chose that moment to return, huffing, "Save the kissy faces for later. We've got company."

# 9
## Typhon

Typhon itched. Not the kind of itching that required him to scratch his flesh but the nagging sense of something amiss. From the moment they'd arrived in Zuzamenn, he'd been bothered.

For one, despite what he'd told the group, they should have been greeted upon arrival by the guardians. They patrolled the miles of wasteland beyond the town, moving from gateway to gateway, guiding visitors, ensuring the wrong sort—a.k.a. invaders—hadn't accidentally found their way over.

It was almost a relief when Enyo stated they had company. Until he saw those riding toward them on the backs of the large lacerlum, which, to those who needed to visualize, resembled a tri-humped lizard with tanned, leathery skin and a long neck.

What disturbed Typhon about their arrival? It wasn't guardians in bronze armor riding the animals but a medley of folk. He spotted a fae female with a nocked bow. A goblin. A dwarf strapped into place since his short legs couldn't hug the lacerlum saddle. A few human types were in there, too. Seven people in all on four mounts.

The dog began yapping. The tiny furball didn't seem to realize one misplaced paw from a lacerlum would crush it.

Deino kept her fingers laced with his, a strange thing to do. For him at least. He knew humans often enjoyed holding on to each other. He'd never had a female before who dared touch him outside of bed. He enjoyed it more than expected.

Frieda and John remained close, as did Enyo, but off to the side in a position of readiness. Only Bane was missing, but not far, Typhon would have wagered.

When the group atop the lacerlum arrived and staggered to a halt, the dog finally quieted and chose to sit on Deino's feet. Typhon readied to greet them, only to have Frieda step forth, hands clasped, with a demure smile. "Greetings. How lovely of you all to come out here to meet us."

The oldest in the group, a grizzled male in mismatched armor, squinted before growling, "Go away."

Unexpected. The few times he'd visited, the guardians had first asked him to state his business.

An undaunted Frieda ignored that request. "We've only just arrived and have business with the oracle."

"The oracle's gone," the grizzled human declared.

The news dropped Typhon's jaw, and he blurted out, "Gone where?"

"Dunno." This time the dwarf replied. "Ain't no one seen her since the attack."

"What attack? What's happened?" Typhon barked out questions. It had been some time since he'd last visited Zuzamenn, and while things could have changed, it surprised. Zuzamenn had long been a place of neutrality.

"The deusvenati came looking for her."

His blood chilled at hearing the name. "How long ago?"

"Couple of days," the grizzled male replied. "They slaughtered the guardians and any folk that got in their way."

"They killed the oracle?" he questioned.

The fae woman shook her head. "We don't know what happened to her other than she's disappeared."

"Why did they go after her?" Typhon asked even as he wondered how the deusvenati managed to surprise the oracle. She should have seen them coming.

"They didn't say why," grumbled the dwarf. "And when they couldn't find her, they took those with magic in their blood."

At the news, Typhon rubbed his face. "Since when do the deusvenati leave their world to meddle in others?" They'd long eschewed trade and even simple communication with what they called the arcane-tainted.

"I'll wager it's that cunt's fault," barked the dwarf. "Coming here, making demands, and when she was told to shove off, she sent back those fuckers."

"By cunt, are we talking about Ariadne? About yay high." Enyo held up her hand. "Thinks she's pretty but she's damned cold.

Likes to wear a crown. Pretends like she's important."

Spears rattled and pointed at the group as the grizzly leader snapped, "What do you know of her?"

Enyo showed no fear as she stepped close to say, "We're looking for Ariadne. She has something of ours, and we're aiming to take it back."

"You're too late. She's long gone," a disgruntled dwarf stated.

"Is she working with the deusvenati?" Typhon clarified. That would be surprising given what he knew of those people. They hated all things magic.

The dwarf shrugged. "Maybe. No one saw her with them during the attack, but given she left town and headed in the direction of the doorway to their world, seems likely."

Not the best news. Typhon addressed the leader. "Back to the oracle, when you say disappeared, was she taken or simply smart enough to go into hiding?"

"Who the fuck knows?" growled the old fellow.

But the fae murmured, "She did give warning."

"Warning?" exclaimed the dwarf. "She told everyone the day before the attack that it might be a good time to go on a holiday."

"She tried to evacuate the town, but no one listened," murmured Frieda.

"She should have told us what was coming and not played word games," argued the dwarf.

To which Frieda replied, "She didn't know what was coming because she couldn't see them."

The explanation actually made a great deal of sense, and so Typhon explained. "The deusvenati are the antithesis to magic. They abhor it and wiped it from their world. They created the collars and matching bands that Ariadne used."

"If they hate magic so much, why create objects to control it?" Deino asked.

"Because, initially, when they revolted against the arcane, they thought to corral it. Only later did their fanaticism evolve to a point where they demanded the eradication of all things magical. However, they didn't used to leave their world to attack the arcane in others." They were fanatics of the worst sort. He'd assumed they'd have died off, given their civilization had begun to spiral around the time he'd gotten incarcerated.

"Who are you that you know so much about them?" the suspicious leader asked.

"Just a traveler." Typhon downplayed his status.

"Travel elsewhere. Zuzamenn is closed for business until further notice." The whiskery male slashed his hand.

"We'll be gone by morning. My companions need to rest." A lie that nobody debunked.

"You'd better leave sooner than later if you know what's good for you. Be a shame if they came after the witches in your group," the dwarf threatened.

With that warning, the party atop the ugly lizards turned around and trotted off. The fae pivoted in the saddle with her nocked bow and watched them. Typhon doubted they'd go far and would likely monitor them until they did indeed leave.

"Well, that fucks our plan to talk to the oracle and find Ariadne," muttered Deino.

"She's not dead," Frieda remarked. "But she is hiding."

"Where?" Typhon asked, not questioning how she knew.

"Not too far. She's injured." Frieda closed her

eyes and lifted her chin. "We need to go that way." She whirled and pointed to the lights of town.

"That can't be right. That bunch of yahoos said she'd disappeared," Deino pointed out.

"Disappeared in plain sight," Enyo surmised. "Smart. She must have a hidey-hole no one knows about."

"Why would she still be hiding if the threat is gone?"

It was Typhon who guessed the answer. "Because the deusvenati most likely threatened those they left alive. My guess? The townsfolk were told to hand over the oracle or those they took would die."

"Meaning there are informants ready to rat if she pops her head out." Enyo sounded agitated. "I hate snitches."

A quiet John finally spoke. "I guess the real question is, do we still need to speak to the oracle? Those people seemed to imply that Ariadne went to wherever these deusvenati came from, meaning we have a location."

"Assuming she stayed there, which doesn't seem likely given these deusvenati don't like magic users," Deino pointed out.

"Maybe we got lucky and they already killed her," John suggested.

Typhon shook his head. "She's alive."

"Personally, I dislike the fact there's a whole town waiting to hand over a woman to save their own asses," Enyo stated and then added, "I, for one, think we should still go and find her."

"Find her how?" Deino asked. "We're being watched, which means we can't exactly walk into town and go poking around for the oracle. Not to mention, if we do locate her, we could end up with a fight on our hands if these people are in contact with those deusvenati and they come back to take her."

"Ooh, fight?" Enyo grinned.

"Not everything has to be a battle," his witch pointed out.

"The deusvenati should not be underestimated," Typhon added. "They are like those things we encountered at the hotel, able to repel magic."

"Bah, those were easy to take out," Enyo scoffed.

"Those creatures weren't trained warriors. The deusvenati are immune to magic. A fight with them might not go as expected."

"Lovely. I finally get the power to make a difference and keep running into people who can counter it." Deino scowled.

"What should we do?" John laid out the most important question.

"There are only two real choices. Leave or find the oracle." Typhon eyed his champions, leaving the choice to them. He recognized entering the town posed a danger but so did leaving without further information.

"Me, I say fuck the snitches. We find the oracle and get her ass out of here," Enyo said.

Deino glanced at Frieda. "What do you see down that path?"

The sister who could see the future pursed her lips. "It's murky, but there is one thing that is clear. We have to go find her."

For some reason, Typhon felt a shiver at her declaration, as if a momentous choice had been made.

He just hoped they didn't regret it.

# 10

"How are we supposed to sneak into the town given we're being watched?" John pointed out the flaw in our decision.

"We can't sneak," I stated. "There's no cover to hide our approach." Then, before Enyo could argue, I added, "And not enough shadows for you to hide in, especially since your giant kitty will want to tag along."

My warrior sister scowled. "Says you."

"Yes, says me. Six people—sorry, five and two furballs—trying to sneak in is going to be noticed."

"She's right," Frieda murmured. "I see no path where we can all go in together."

"Bullshit," huffed Enyo. "If those idiots are the best this town's got, I can take them."

"Don't be so dramatic." I snorted. "No need to kill folk just trying to protect what's left. And I didn't say it was impossible, only that we're too many. Which is why, while John puts up a camouflage to make it hard to see what we're doing, I'll go in. I can float above the ground and use a mirror shield to cover me."

"To land where?" Enyo crossed her arms. "If those town folk can't find the oracle, what makes you think you can fly your ass in and locate her?"

"Because she'll be taking me with her." Frieda's reply caused pandemonium, with John bellowing almost as loud as Enyo.

"Like fuck!" My sister and John agreed, while Frieda looked stubborn and determined. An expression and attitude I was still getting used to.

The monster god remained quiet, and it was to him I looked. "You haven't said much."

"What is there to say? You are right. We can't walk into the town. You can't find the oracle on your own. Your plan seems to be the only feasible one unless someone would like to offer another."

Everyone eyed each other, but no one actually had a thing to say, leading to me clapping my hands. "Then it's settled. Me and French fry will go in and locate the oracle, make the bargain, get our info, and then rejoin the group so we can portal out." My simple plan had Typhon nodding, but John shook his head.

"You make it sound easy, but what if you're caught?"

"Then we fight." I shrugged. "I won't start it, but if I'm attacked, I will end it."

"If that happens, you send me a message." Enyo stared at me, and I nodded. I'd use our triplet bond to notify her. Knowing my sister, she wouldn't be far.

A glance at Typhon showed him looking pensive. "What's up, Ty? Got anything to add?"

"Be careful with the oracle."

I grinned. "Better watch out or I'll start thinking you care."

He grimaced. "You make light, but I do have a concern. If she is desperate, she might make an unreasonable request."

"Then we say no. I'm good at doing that." Just ask the guys who hit on me.

While Frieda went off a few paces to murmur and exchange kisses with John, Enyo went back into the shadows, most likely to rejoin Bane.

I moved close to Typhon and muttered, "Any last words of advice?"

"Don't die."

I snickered. "That's the plan." I peeked at him through my lashes. "Think you can survive without me?"

"I'll do my best," was his dry reply.

On impulse, I floated up until we were eye level and brushed a kiss against his lips, whispering, "For luck."

I didn't expect the arms that crushed me against him and the hard mouth that slanted against mine, taking my luck and turning it into a heart-pounding embrace. When he set me on my feet, I almost touched my tingling lips. Wow. I didn't let my pleasure show.

With my nonchalance in place, I winked and said, "Can't wait to see what I get when I return victorious."

"Just come back," he growled.

Frieda joined me, still frail-looking, but I knew better now. She had a core of steel, and when she grabbed hold of my hand, she was the one to say, "Let's get this show on the road."

"Don't you mean sky?" I teased as my magic enveloped us. We rose, leaving Typhon and John behind, a shield already in place that made it seem like the entire party was there, including my dog, who'd been behaving better than usual and seemed to have taken a shine to Typhon. Like mistress, like pet, I guess.

I turned my focus from them to the task at hand. My magic floated my sister and me over the land with ease, my mirror shield reflecting what was on the other side of us, making it an almost seamless view to anyone looking at us from below. I spotted the self-appointed guardians not too far from our group. None of them once looked up or realized we'd slipped past.

We moved quickly in the windless sky that went from day to night startlingly quick. As we neared the town, I noticed that while lights shone from lampposts that marked the winding streets, not a single house showed even a crack of illumination. While early, it could be that everyone had gone to sleep. What surprised? The lack of sentries. For a town recently attacked, I'd have expected a few folks parked out on rooftops keeping watch. Then again, could be I just didn't spot or sense them. A sobering reminder that I might not be as clever as I thought.

I asked my sister, "Where to?"

"The bakery."

"You do recall those folks said she wasn't home."

"Trust me."

"Which one's the bakery?" I asked as we passed over the first rooftop, a mishmash of materials: wood, thatch, even plates of metal. The buildings themselves appeared mostly made of stone with the doors ranging from planked wood to ornately adorned metal. All the windows appeared heavily shuttered.

Frieda suddenly pointed, and a second later, I noticed the dangling sign with a loaf of bread. We'd found the bakery.

The oracle lived above it, according to Typhon, and so I aimed for a closed window. Only Frieda hissed, "Stop. We can't go through there. It's trapped."

I wanted to slap myself for not looking first. Had I peeked at all, I would have seen the strands of magic stretching over the frame and the shutters.

Rather than ask Frieda how to get in, I landed us atop the roof, the overlapping clay tiles solid to stand on. Also easy to remove.

"Keep to the side," I warned my sister as I

knelt and began tracing a section with my finger. I shaped my magic into that tip, imagining it cutting the tile, but also holding the pieces I cut so that they didn't fall and make a ruckus below. It took some concentration to remove the tiles piece by piece. I was almost done when Frieda murmured, "Hurry up. Someone's coming up the road."

Startled, I acted a little too quickly, and a single tile escaped, falling with a thud below.

I froze.

Frieda put a hand on my arm, and we stared over the edge of the roof. A man, carrying a studded bat, paused. He glanced left and right. Even up. I had a mirage shield in place ensuring he saw only a bare roof and a single missing tile to explain the one on the ground.

He kicked it, frowned, looked up again. Seeing nothing, he continued on his way.

I finished my hole and cast out a scan for anyone inside the apartment. When the ping returned confirming it was empty, I floated my sister down then myself.

The room we entered had obviously been tossed for clues. What once might have been a cute apartment, trashed. Pillows ripped apart.

Furniture turned over. Ceramic pots broken and their contents strewn.

I tsked. "Did they think she hid in a container?"

"This was anger that she slipped their grip," Frieda replied.

"Where did she go?"

My sister glanced at me. "Nowhere. Can't you feel it? She's still here."

I glanced around the single room. Even the bathroom area had no walls to hide its butt pot, larger tub for bathing, and bowl for a sink. "Did she shrink to be ant-sized? Because I don't see anyone."

"For a witch, you're not very smart. Think. If you didn't have time to escape your place and needed to hide, what would you do?"

"Kill a lot of people while screaming freedom?"

Frieda snickered. "Yeah, you probably would. So let's say it was me, and you, being a witch, wanted me safe. You'd build me—"

"A safe room." Frieda had one to help her against the noise of the world. Only... "Still not seeing where it would be. There's no attic, and the shop is right below this floor." I didn't sense any magic either, other than the trap on the windows and the hatch for the stairs.

"Good thing I came along," my sister grumbled as she headed for a tapestry hanging drunkenly on the wall. She ripped it aside, and before I could say a word, she stepped through the wall.

# 11
## Typhon

Typhon hated waiting. He hated not knowing. Hated being as weak as a mortal. But most of all, he hated seeing Deino go off without him.

The dog whined. He glanced down at it. "Yeah, I'm not pleased with the situation either."

John didn't find it odd he spoke to the dog. That, or he assumed Typhon addressed him. "We can get closer to the town if you want. I can have the illusion move with us."

"Won't they notice we've shifted position?" Typhon asked.

John pointed. "Pretty sure our watchers are heading back."

Sure enough, a glance and a squint showed the self-appointed guardians heading for the town.

"Did they leave someone behind to spy on us?"

"Maybe. Do you care?" John asked.

"No. Let's get closer." The nagging sensation of something amiss refused to leave. With the dog hugging his heels, Typhon matched his pace to John's, his gaze scanning. Not that he could sense much. He could only assume Enyo was nearby. The warrior truly blended well with shadows, to the point even if right in front of her, he couldn't spot her.

Annoying. He had to wonder what else he couldn't see with his mundane senses.

The professor of the arcane didn't say much, which Typhon appreciated, seeing as how he dealt with a strange new feeling.

Worry. Not for himself. For his witch.

He didn't like she'd gone off without him even as he recognized her plan as the best one. It bothered him she'd be without his protection even as she was more capable of protecting herself right now than he was. Most of all, he hated the feeling of anticipation in the air. A sense of impending trouble. They should have left the moment they heard about the deusvenati. They should have left once they realized the oracle couldn't be spoken with. But to go where?

Knowing Ariadne worked with the deusvenati —willingly or not—changed everything and nothing. If she was with them, getting to her would be almost impossible. At the same time, until he could have her release his power, he'd be useless. What choice did he have?

It shouldn't have surprised—but it did irritate —that his release from his prison was fraught with complications. He'd assumed once he'd escaped he'd find Ariadne and, poof, he'd be a powerful god again. Instead, he'd been beset with problems. Not all of them bad. The witch proved to be more delightful than he'd have expected.

She'd kissed him before leaving. Kissed him, and when he'd been unable to resist and kissed her back, had mentioned something about more later.

Had she not heard him when he said getting involved was a bad idea? Although he couldn't articulate why, unless it was the fear of letting her get close. It had been a long time since his last emotional attachment. It didn't end well. None of them ever did. The whole problem with being a god. Either they wanted something from him or they feared him. No one ever just loved him.

John nudged Typhon's arm and pointed to their left.

Caught up in his maudlin musings, he'd missed the fact they'd caught up to the group that warned them earlier. They appeared to be arguing amongst themselves.

They remained hidden behind John's illusion, but just in case, Typhon unleashed his cloak, the billowy fabric forming a shadowy cover that encompassed John and the dog. The wizard must have done something to enhance sound, because he suddenly could hear them talking.

"...should have let them go to town instead of telling them to leave," said the one with blond whiskers.

"We're just handing magic users over to the deusvenati now?" scoffed the bald fellow.

"It's called keeping them happy so they give back our families," grumbled Whiskers.

"Not by sacrificing innocent travelers," the fae woman argued.

"Better them than us," insisted Baldy.

"Would be better if it was no one at all," insisted the dwarf. "Can't believe the oracle didn't see them coming."

"She must have. How else did she know to hide?" a sour Whiskers stated.

"I heard they found blood in her place. Maybe she's dead," Baldy offered.

"Then where's her body?" countered the fae.

"I don't know. Maybe it turned to dust. She is really old, after all." Bald man had an explanation.

"The deusvenati seem to think she's still alive."

"The deusvenati can suck my dick," Baldy insulted.

"You'll get to ask them soon enough," Whiskers stated.

"Wait, have you heard something? Are they supposed to return soon?" The fae woman sounded worried.

"Those travelers should have left when they had the chance. By now, the hunters are aware of them."

Typhon stiffened.

"How? Ain't none of us returned to town yet," the dwarf reminded.

"You think that matters?" Whiskers scoffed.

"Maybe we should have let them go looking for the oracle," mused Baldy.

"You gonna hand her over?" snapped the dwarf.

"If it keeps me and my family alive, yes," Baldy stated with no shame.

"You're an arsehole," the fae woman declared. "I'm done with you lot. I'm going home to pack and get out of here."

"Me too," said the dwarf. The pair of them headed off, sharing a lumbering beast, while the remaining humans eyed each other.

Baldy pursed his lips. "Maybe it is time to move. Somewhere with less shit to deal with."

"Where?"

"I hear Earth is an interesting place," was the last thing they heard as the last of the group began walking toward town, holding the tethers of their beasts.

John waited a moment before whispering, "Not a happy bunch."

"Can't blame them. They went from a peaceful existence to one threatened."

"You think someone ratted us out to these deusvenati?" John asked.

"Yes." Typhon stood. His cloak rippled despite the lack of breeze. He glanced around.

"What's wrong?"

He couldn't articulate it other than a sense of wrongness. "Something's not right."

The dog sensed it, too, rising to its four stubby legs and whimpering. Typhon pursed his lips before snaring Jinx and murmuring, "Let's put you somewhere safe. I have a feeling things are going to get difficult." He tucked the dog inside the satchel with its extra dimension of space. The mongrel would be protected, which, while not important to him—in his time dogs served a purpose and it wasn't as an accessory—he knew would matter a lot to Deino. For some reason, he cared about that.

He slung the bag across his shoulders, and the cloak re-formed over it. John eyed him. "You're expecting trouble."

"I think we should go find our women."

"That patrol isn't far ahead of us."

He glanced at John. "That's unfortunate for them. If they're smart, they'll stay out of our way. I have a feeling Deino and Frieda are going to need us."

"Then let's get moving." John adopted a rapid

pace that Typhon matched. The town neared enough for him to make out details, including the fact the human part of the patrol had arrived.

A sudden stillness in the air paused him.

"What's happening?" John murmured as the air became charged with static.

"A portal is opening."

Not unusual in a nexus place like Zuzamenn with permanent doorways that didn't require users to have magic. Typhon didn't start running —and worrying—until he heard someone scream, "The deusvenati have returned!"

# 12

Frieda stepped into the wall but didn't smash her face or bounce. She disappeared, and I felt like the dumbest witch.

A pocket dimension panic room. How fucking brilliant. How had I not thought of it? How was it I couldn't sense the magic tethering it in place?

I quickly followed my sister, passing through the wall to find myself in—a garden?

I'll admit it took me a second of gaping before I recovered my wits.

The oasis had much greenery—trees, bushes, flowers—so much of it I couldn't see if there was a sky. I did hear water, which came from a pond being fed by a creek. Lovely and peaceful with signs of habitation. A table with two chairs, holding a tea set. A chest with fabric pushing up the lid. Urns and crates. But the thing that drew the eye and held it? The old woman lying prone on a hammock. Frieda stood by her side, holding her hand.

"She's hurt," my sister announced.

"No shit." I could smell the blood and rot from here.

As I neared the oracle, I didn't need a doctor's degree to know the situation didn't look good. Beneath the many wrinkles, the woman's skin tone appeared ashen and her lips dry. She barely breathed, and she certainly didn't react to my sister clutching her hand.

"She's dying," I announced as if it weren't obvious.

"Can you fix her?" asked Frieda.

"I'm not a healer." My magic could break things, but fixing? Not part of my skill set.

"We have to help her," my sister insisted.

"I'm open to suggestions." I tugged at the cloth crusted with yellow and brown. It peeled away, and a stench exhaled from the wound that made my stomach turn. Frieda turned aside and retched.

I eyed the injury in the oracle's flesh. She'd been stabbed in the gut and the edges of it festered, the skin turning black, the hole itself oozing something that smelled rancid. Rot had set in, and I feared by the smell something vital was perforated.

"Maybe if we cleaned and cauterized it?" Frieda suggested.

"Nothing can fix this." Even if I could have rushed her to a hospital, she'd die.

But Frieda, my kind sister, wanted to help. "We have to do something." She tore a strip from the blanket dangling off the hammock and soaked it in the creek, pressing the damp fabric against the oozing sore. A useless gesture but I said nothing.

The oracle woke with a gasp, her body slightly bowing, her lips parting. But what staggered me? The eyes. They had no iris, no pupil, just a pure yellow glow, like two suns.

Uncanny? You have no idea.

A frail voice emerged. "I've waited a long time to meet the sisters."

"Which is weird because we just heard about you hours ago." My probably not-so-nice reply.

"The prophecy gathers speed," whispered the oracle. "The beginning of the end now starts."

Great. A ranting oracle. What a waste of a trip.

Frieda returned with a basin for more dabbing, only to have the oracle slap her hand. "It's too late for that. The poison on the deusvenati blade cannot be cured without drastic measure."

"Is that a polite way of saying we should let you die?" I didn't cushion my words.

The oracle snorted. "Death, ha. I would have become dust if you'd not come, but now that you're here, the prophecy foretold unfolds as it should. As I predicted."

Given she seemed willing to talk, I had to ask. "Do you know where Ariadne is? The twat who stole the monster god's magic?"

"She is with the godless."

"The godless being?" I asked to be sure.

"The deusvenati who wish to eradicate all gods and their blessings."

"Let me guess, so that only their god is left?" Because every religion I'd ever heard of remained convinced theirs was the only true path with the one true god.

"They have no god. They killed him long ago and have since regretted it, which is why they've been trying to bring him back."

"By killing magic?"

"Never said it made sense."

"Sounds like a recipe for the zombie apocalypse." My bedside manner could probably use work.

"They will destroy all life if allowed to proceed with their current plan," gasped the old woman. "But the prophecy states you will stop it."

"Great. And how are we supposed to do that?" Clear-cut instructions would be nice.

"The sisters must prevail."

"Ah, because that makes it so clear." I rolled my eyes.

"Be nice and listen," Frieda chided.

"How do we win against these deusvenati, find Ariadne, give Typhon back his power, and get back home all in one piece?" I fired a boatload of questions in hope of one not-so-useless reply.

"You must go to their world."

"Of course we do." I rubbed my forehead. "And let me guess, it's going to be dangerous." I mean a place with arcane hunters and magic-cancelling collars... What could go wrong?

"A mortal shall enter but not return," the oracle confirmed.

The ominous announcement had me glaring. "What's that supposed to mean? Who's *not* returning?" Of our group, no one was expendable. My sisters? No fucking way. Their partners? They'd probably snap a gasket. Which left Typhon... I was oddly reluctant for him to be killed, although the word mortal did imply it wouldn't be him.

"Quickly. We don't have much time," the old woman declared.

"Time for what?"

"Your sister knows." The oracle gripped Frieda's hand. "When Apate came and asked for my advice so long ago, I had only one price."

My blood chilled as my sister looked at me with apology.

"What are you talking about? What did Mom bargain?" I tried to gather my magic but, in that moment, realized it wouldn't come to me in this place. Something muffled it. Mine, at any rate. The oracle, on the other hand, began to glow, and that glow started riding up my sister's arm.

"Apate wanted to know how to right a grievous wrong. The future needed heroes, and I needed an heir," was the breathy whisper. "It took careful planning to get to this point that the gift might pass on."

Before I could tell the old lady to fuck off, Frieda went rigid. Her head tilted back, her mouth opening wide as the light enveloped them both.

I would have physically torn them apart, but the nimbus surrounding them repelled my attempts to shove past it. Screaming and pummeling did nothing. It resisted my efforts.

It didn't last long—despite the eternity in my emotions. The magical light faded, and the old oracle was gone. In her place was a young woman with a scar on her abdomen, wearing stained rags.

Frieda gasped and staggered from the hammock. Alive. For now. But I could see she'd changed. Not so much in appearance but aura. She glowed much brighter than before.

"French fry!" I cried as I grabbed her. "Are you okay?"

"I will be," she murmured.

"The gift has been passed on. My role is done." The young woman rose from the hammock and flicked her hand at us. "Time for you to go and fulfill your destiny. To forge a new prophecy. A fresh future."

"Oh no you don't. I think you owe us some answers, lady," I protested, but the words got sucked away by the storm-grade wind that pushed at Frieda and me, whipping us into retreat until we popped out of the wall into the destroyed room.

I stared at the wall in disbelief. How dare she!

"Like fuck, lady." I ran for the doorway, only to yelp as I hit solid stone. Frieda caught my ricocheting ass.

"She's gone, Dina. And we have to go too."

I shoved out of my sister's grip and scowled. "What did she do to you?"

"Gave me a purpose for my powers."

"Meaning what?"

Frieda turned a cheeky smile on me. "Meaning you need to be nice to the new oracle."

She seemed pleased, so I gave her a reality check. "You mean she put a target on your back. Those deusvenati want the oracle."

"I'm aware, which is why we have to leave." Rather than take our rooftop exit, she headed for the stairs, and I only had a second to deactivate the magical alarm before she descended to the main level of the shop.

"Can you see them? Are the bad guys coming?" I asked as I trailed behind.

"I cannot see who they are outside of magic."

"So that's a no on seeing the magic-killers coming. Great," I huffed. "Guess this means you can't see what happens if we confront them on their world."

"Not we. You. This is where our journey diverges," she announced as she tugged at the door leading outside.

"What do you mean diverges? I'm not going anywhere without you," I stated as we spilled into the street.

Frieda clasped my hands. "It will be okay. I understand now."

"Understand what? Because I sure as fuck don't," I grumbled.

"It's okay, dear sister. I know you're afraid."

"Am not." And that wasn't a lie. Pissed. Annoyed. Murderous. Those better described my state of mind.

"You have a great destiny if you don't fuck up."

I blinked. "What's that supposed to mean?"

"You've been closed off since *his* death." He being my fiancé who died of cancer.

"And?"

"And it's time you started to live again. Love again. Oh, and don't be afraid to kick some ass."

"Hold on. Let's go back to this love thing. I don't need a man to make me happy," I argued.

She patted my hand. "Sure you don't. Because your vibrator is great at cuddling."

"You cunt muffin. Take that back!" I huffed.

"Save the name-calling for later. They're here." She turned from me to smile as John and Typhon came jogging into view.

John, a blond professor with tousled hair and a bright smile for his wife.

Typhon, a vengeful, stalking shadow with a billowing cloak and grim expression. It was as sexy as you'd expect.

"We have company," Typhon announced.

"So I hear. Where are they?" I asked. "And where's Enyo?" I sent a mental poke, *Sis? We have bogeys incoming.*

*Shh. I'm busy.*

My lips pinched. Enyo was hunting. Good and not good. We couldn't escape without her and her furball.

John scooped Frieda up and swung her around for a kiss.

Typhon glowered. But then again, so did I. "Where's my dog?"

He patted the satchel. "Tucked away to keep her out of trouble."

Not a bad idea. "Where are the bad guys?" I asked just as a scream erupted in the distance.

"I'd say over there," was Typhon's cheeky reply.

"Any plans on how to kill them? Aren't they supposedly immune to magic?"

"You'll have to stab them with a heavy sword or sharp spear. Nothing else will penetrate their armor," he advised.

"What about bullets?"

He shrugged. "They didn't have any in my time, but one would assume they should work."

I hated assumptions. I also hated the fact I didn't have a weapon. But my bag did. I crouched and dropped my satchel on the ground and shoved in my arm up to the shoulder, feeling around. Huge fucking thing made it hard to find anything.

The wet lick might have startled me if I'd not been the recipient of Jinx's love. I gave her a scratch and murmured, "Hi, baby. Momma needs a weapon." My dog, the smartest one alive, emerged from the bag, dragging a revolver. "Thanks, baby." I might not have Enyo's aim, but I could hit a target well enough.

"Got anything else in there?" Typhon asked.

I felt around even as Frieda stated, "There's no point in arming ourselves. We won't win if we take a stand. We have to go. Now."

"But Enyo and Bane aren't here," I pointed out.

"Too late," Typhon muttered. "They're coming."

At his words, I rose from my crouch and stared at the approaching menace.

I don't know what I expected. I mean with a name like deusvenati, I'd kind of pictured something from *Lord of the Rings*. You know giant, ugly orcs or something a little more ephemeral like the dementors in Harry Potter.

Instead, I got knights. Six feet tall or more, wearing golden-hued armor head to toe, bearing swords that gleamed wetly, the tips of them showing a sticky substance, most likely poison.

A group of five, they didn't run, they didn't yell. They marched toward us in unison.

*Thump. Thump.* I kind of expected the ground to shake with each booted step. Only my bravery quivered at their approach.

I lifted my fingers, ready to bowl them over with a bowling ball of air, but Typhon grabbed my hand. "They're immune to magic."

"They might be, but the ground isn't," I countered, ripping my hand free and aiming my concentrated power at the ground under their feet.

The magic shot from my fingers and hit the cobbled road, jiggling the stones loose and nothing more, although the deusvenati did glow for a few seconds.

I gaped. "Those fuckers ate my spell."

"I warned you," Typhon growled. "You can't defeat them with magic."

Fine. I aimed the gun in my hand and fired. A perfect shot. It hit one of the golden knights in the chest with a ping. The bullet fell to the ground.

"Uh-oh," I muttered.

"Die, fuckers!" Enyo dove from above, a Valkyrie with no wings, her long sword extended. The knight she went after barely had time to react, lifting his arm to shield, and losing it.

"Yay!" Yes, I cheered.

My sister began to clang her weapon against the knight who, despite losing an arm, seemed determined to fight. Of interest, blue blood ran liberally from the stump.

Cool.

Of concern? How the other knights began closing in on my sister.

"We have to do something!" I yelled.

Typhon sighed. "A god isn't supposed to be a hero. People are supposed to be heroic in his name." He complained, and yet he moved toward the golden group, a long dagger in hand, his cloak floating around him.

John ignored Frieda's clutching hands and, with his own blade, strode to join him.

An unhappy Frieda hissed, "Do something."

"Like what?" I snapped back. "Can't use the gun. Can't use my magic. Would you like me to sing?" Being tone-deaf led to me being banned from doing Karaoke.

"Send us back to the portal for Earth. They're forbidden from following," Frieda stated.

I wanted to ask how she knew that, only I got distracted by Enyo's cry of pain. Which led to the giant kitty roaring as he raced up the road. He soared for the knight who dared to draw blood from his mate. Surely those big, powerful jaws could crush the tin-canned soldiers?

A golden glove grabbed at the leopard, and suddenly a naked Bane dangled from his grip. Even shifter magic was affected.

This was bad. So bad. We couldn't win. Time to take Frieda's advice.

"John, get ready to grab Frieda and go," I hollered as I concentrated my magic and used it to rip open a doorway that would set them just outside the portal to Earth.

Frieda gave me the most serene look before her husband tossed her over his shoulder. I heard her in my head, *You've got this, sis.*

Fucking right I did.

John, holding his wife, leaped into the portal.

One sister down.

The other did her best to keep the blades at bay, but without her magical strength and other abilities, she tired, and her flesh showed stripes that dripped red.

Bane didn't fare any better. The bloodied man got tossed, and he hit the pavement hard and slid. Ouch. Road rash.

A mighty blow to Enyo sent her staggering, and she chose to regroup by Bane's side.

This was my chance. "Get your ass in the portal, Yo-yo!" I yelled, straining to keep the doorway open.

Enyo's lips went flat. "You first. I'll cover the retreat."

Fucking hell. Why did she love me so much?

With one part of me concentrating on the doorway, another part bubbled my sister and Bane and tossed them into the portal.

My dog chose that moment to bravely bark as the deusvenati headed in my direction. "Sorry, baby. Go wait for me with your aunties." I sent Jinx through the doorway and bit my lip as I strained to keep the portal open.

"Typhon! We have to go," I hollered as the man continued to fight, his bladework impeccable. He spun it round and round, a dervish that didn't need magic to fight.

But I did. I felt myself growing weak. Too weak to hold the portal open when I had to dodge a strike.

I stumbled and fell to the ground, losing my grip on the doorway and uttering a groan at the realization I didn't have the strength to open another. Not that it would matter, as the golden knight standing over me would kill me in just a second.

Only the death blow never arrived.

To my surprise, sudden hollers showed reinforcements had arrived. The dwarf we'd met earlier came bellowing with an axe. His mighty swing took out my wannabe killer at the knees. As I pushed to my feet, I couldn't help but gape in surprise as arrows struck, poking holes in the armor of the deusvenati.

From the shuttered houses crept the townspeople, clutching weapons, expressions grim.

One woman with a large butcher knife screamed, "You killed my husband and daughter." Then charged.

Others joined.

In the chaos, Typhon slipped to my side and wrapped an arm around my weak body. "We have to get you away," he stated as he dragged us from the main battle into a spot between buildings.

"I don't think I can open another doorway," I gasped. I could barely keep my eyes open as overexertion pulled at every single limb.

"We'll never make it to the doorway without being caught. We need a place to hide."

"Where? We're in an alien place with people who might just decide we're not worth the trouble and turn us in." I wanted to laugh hysterically.

"Somewhere safe. Somewhere safe," he muttered before the light bulb hit. I could see it in the way his expression brightened, and he grimaced. "I have an idea. Possibly a bad one." He dumped the satchel he'd grabbed during our escape.

"I'm sure your idea is better than mine because I've got nothing."

He opened the bag. "Crawl in."

I blinked. "Excuse me?"

"Get in the bag," he snapped. "We don't have much time."

I wanted to argue, only I remembered the oracle and how she'd hidden. "Will we both fit?" The opening was large enough for me, but Typhon? He was a big man.

"Guess we'll find out. Now go."

I'll admit I felt a little like that mime who pretended to climb down some stairs, only in this case, I stepped into my bag and plummeted several feet before hitting with an oomph.

"Move aside. I'm coming in."

I scrambled in the dark, not sure of the dimensions. My fingers caught in the jumble of stuff I'd packed. I heard fabric protest and tear, and then what little light we had was gone.

I was still trying to orient myself when Typhon said, "And now we wait."

"How long?" I asked.

I couldn't see, but I imagined him shrugging in the darkness when he replied, "If we're not discovered in the next day, I'd say it worked."

"Day?" I might have squeaked. "What are we supposed to do in the meantime?"

"Rest," he suggested.

Not a bad idea, but because I didn't like the dark, I crawled and felt around me until my hands hit a leg. His leg.

I yanked at him. "Get down here."

"Why?" he asked as he sat beside me.

"Because I'm tired, and you're the only mattress around," I advised as I crawled into his lap.

He could have argued or tossed me to the floor of my satchel, but instead, he cradled me, whispering, "Rest, my witch. I'll guard your sleep."

# 13
## Typhon

Hiding. Not a new thing for Typhon. He'd spent much of his exile staying out of harm's way, for the place he'd found himself had many monsters, none willing to obey a god without powers. He'd hoped his days of scurrying for cover were done. But here he was, once more burrowing in the hopes of surviving until the morrow.

One big difference? He'd never hidden with someone before. Never had anyone trust him with their life. Holding his witch, he found himself awash in feelings. First and foremost, a desire to protect. She felt so small against him. Her frame was tiny compared to his, even as her personality was huge. So much power and sass packed in one body. Her bravery in the face of danger awed. So many would have thrown themselves prostrate and begged for mercy. His witch preferred spitting in death's eye.

He stroked a hand down her back and wondered at the strange fate that brought them together. A fate that would likely tear them apart.

Climbing into the dimension sewn into the satchel had been a last-ditch effort. He didn't actually think it would work. At any moment, he expected someone to open the bag and reach in to drag them out.

At least they'd try.

He'd brought the short sword he'd been using in battle with him and would lop off any limbs that attempted to grab. So far, they'd been undisturbed. A good sign? He had no way of knowing. He didn't dare use any magic for seeing. Bad enough the satchel exuded a faint trace the deusvenati might sniff out.

In good news, technically they could survive a period of time in here. They had some food. Weapons. Clothing. They only really lacked bed and bathing facilities. Hopefully they would be out of here before the latter became an issue. The question being, how long they should wait? He'd said a day. A day would be enough for the deusvenati to lose interest or for someone to claim the bag.

Once they did emerge, they would have to plan their next move. He'd not had a chance to find out what happened with Frieda and Deino's mission to find the oracle, although he noticed the former had a new glow about her. What had happened?

He was tempted to wake his witch, but he ignored the urge. In his former life as a god, he would have demanded an answer and not been willing to wait for it. But this Typhon, the one who'd spent a long time waiting for his chance to return to his life, understood patience.

With nothing else to do, he snuggled his witch, and despite meaning to keep watch, he fell asleep.

He woke to his witch nibbling his jawline. Perhaps she dreamed.

He cleared his throat to wake her. "Hello."

"Morning, Ty. Or should I say afternoon? I have no idea what time it is," she purred against his skin as she shifted her body. Not off him, he should add, but plastering herself more thoroughly against him. He'd lain down at some point and she'd used him as a mattress.

"How are you feeling?" he asked, hoping conversation would provide a distraction because now that she'd regained consciousness, he became all too aware of her.

"Horny," she admitted with no hesitation or shame. "You?"

No point in denying what she probably felt pressing against her. "This probably isn't a good time to indulge in carnal acts."

She chuckled against his neck where she'd moved her lips that continued their nibbling tease. "We're hiding in a dark room, waiting to see if we'll be discovered and killed. If we're not, we then need to sneak out of my oversized purse without being noticed, call a portal, and get our asses out of here to somewhere we will most likely be targeted again. Because, hello, my new life involves a lot of running. So excuse me if I'm going to take my pleasure when and where it can be found." She began kissing his neck, teasing his flesh, and he found it hard to come up with a reason why they should stop.

"Getting involved is probably not a good idea."

"So you say, and yet, from where I'm lying, I'm thinking it's going to be great." She wiggled.

He almost let out an ungodly groan. "You make it hard to say no."

"Then don't. I could use some fun, and so could you." She then kissed him, her sensual touch stronger than any argument. And really, why did he argue?

He wanted her.

He returned her embrace, their lips sliding and teasing, their bodies pressed tight and yet impeded by fabric. It had been a long time since he'd removed his robe. Why would he when it never got dirty or wet?

But he commanded it to part, leaving him naked to her touch, the friction of her garments exquisite torture.

"Undress me," she commanded as she rolled off him.

"Bossy witch," he grumbled as his hands roamed her body, tugging at her clothing, her shirt first then her brassiere. He took his time dragging down her pants and undergarments. While they had no light, he could feel. Feel the smoothness of her skin. The way she shivered and undulated at his touch.

Smell her desire.

He nudged her legs apart that he might cup her mound, the dampness of it making him want to cover her body with his and thrust.

But a god should have more control.

He lay alongside her, and while he traced her damp slit with his finger, he found her earlobe and sucked.

"Mmm." She hummed and rolled her hips, pushing her sex against his hand.

Her molten honey had him salivating for the first time in what seemed like forever. And he couldn't resist.

He shifted himself to a spot between her legs and placed his mouth on her, delighting in her cry of surprise then her moan of pleasure as he licked at her. Tasted her. Indulged in an ambrosia that satisfied him more than anything he'd ever known.

As his tongue teased her swollen button, he inserted a finger and stroked her, feeling the pulsing heat as her pleasure coiled. He put in a second finger, and she squeezed him.

Tight.

Oh, so tight. He began thrusting his digits,

and her hips joined him in the rhythm, pushing him deep, but not deep enough.

Her breathing hitched as she gasped, "I want you inside me."

"Not yet." He kept pumping her with his fingers even as his tongue traced her sex. He flicked it against her clit before he sucked it, pinching it with his lips until she arched with a cry. Her orgasm had her shuddering, her sex squeezing his fingers.

But he didn't stop. While she was in the throes, he kept teasing her until she practically sobbed. "Fuck me."

He could deny her and himself no longer. He covered her body with his. Her legs parted wide to accommodate. He wrapped an arm around her waist, angling her as the tip of his cock teased her sex.

"Don't you dare take it slow," she growled. Her legs wrapped around his hips and tightened, pulling him into her.

His turn to groan.

It had been so long since he'd been intimate. But that didn't explain why this felt so good.

His lips found hers as he fully sheathed himself. Her channel stretched to accommodate and yet remained tight.

Deliciously so.

He began to move, slowly at first, his hips barely shifting. But she dug her nails into his shoulders and urged him, "Faster. Harder."

At her request, he thrust deeper, feeling the suction as he pulled out and the welcome squeeze when he slammed back in.

Deep.

Hard.

Slam.

He'd have sworn she got tighter with every strike to her sweet spot.

So tight.

She rocked in time with his motion, her legs a vise around him that wouldn't let go. When she came, he felt it in every inch of his being.

A rippling wave that pulsed against his cock. That fisted and drew out his own orgasm, wringing him of pleasure, leaving him limp.

A weak and satiated god collapsed atop her. She didn't protest but hugged him tight.

"Think anyone heard me scream?" she murmured.

"A good thing we're in this alternate dimension, or we might have garnered an audience," was his wry yet very pleased reply. Nice to know the pleasure experienced wasn't one-sided.

"Would we notice if someone moved the satchel?" she asked.

"No. And don't ask me how that works," he warned.

She chuckled. "Spoilsport."

He remained buried in her, content, and yet he knew the moment couldn't last. "We should probably get dressed," he said without much feeling behind it.

"Why would we do that when we're just going to get naked again?"

Before he could ask what she meant, she'd pushed him to his back and grabbed hold, stroking his semi-hard cock into readiness.

"I see you still have the stamina of a god. Good. Because it's been a while for me."

She teased him before she rode him, and he couldn't resist using a sliver of magic to create enough light to see her bouncing atop his body, her head thrown back, hair dangling down her back. Her breasts bounced with each motion. His hands on her hips helped to rock her as she panted and rode him to orgasm.

A climax he shared. His fingers dug into her flesh as he spilled for a second time then lay there gasping, spent.

She leaned down to kiss him. "That should hold me for a few hours. Let's get dressed and go fuck with the outside world."

She stood, and he suddenly understood why some people loved to worship because looking at her, powerful and beautiful—*mine*—he wanted nothing more than to lay every single world at her feet.

He might have started with Zuzamenn, only when they emerged it was to find the town utterly destroyed.

# 14

I emerged to find death all around. While we'd been tucked inside my oversized purse—having epic sex—the town had been destroyed.

The buildings remained mostly standing but heavily damaged. Fire scorched the walls and had turned to ash the parts that weren't stone. Doors, shutters, roofs, all gone, leaving Zuzamenn a shell of what it used to be.

But worse than the destruction of property? The bodies strewn where they'd fallen. The dwarf who'd come to our aid just outside the bakery, half burnt, but I recognized his long beard and the axe he still clutched. The fae woman lay on the cobblestones, face first, a viscous pool of blood spreading from her head.

Every step I took showed a new atrocity. My fault. Maybe if I'd not told my sisters to run and I'd not hidden, we could have made a difference. But we'd been cowards, thinking only of ourselves. We'd left these people to fend for themselves, and they died because of it.

I didn't even realize I'd gathered magic to me until Typhon murmured, "You're not to blame for this."

"How do you figure that?" I demanded as I whirled. My magic swirled with me, whipping my hair in a wild storm that only affected me. "We came here and drew the deusvenati."

"Not true. They had already been by before our arrival. They returned because they'd not gotten what they wanted."

"They wanted the oracle." I uttered a bitter laugh. "A woman who would have died probably within hours if we'd not interfered."

"What happened? You saw her?"

We'd not spoken of what I'd seen and heard. Too busy resting and then taking our pleasure while others suffered. A part of me knew staying would have led to me dying, but it didn't assuage my guilt. "We found the oracle grievously injured and hidden inside a pocket dimension, but one much nicer than my purse." I grimaced. "She was dying. Poisoned by a deusvenati blade. Her flesh rotting."

"Did she speak before her demise?"

"She didn't die. She'd been awaiting our arrival." My lips pinched as I remembered her rambling. "She mentioned something about the beginning of the end. Told us we had to confront the deusvenati on their world but not everyone would go home." Part of the reason why I panicked and sent my sisters fleeing. My head ducked. "The oracle grabbed hold of my sister and cursed her, transferring the oracle thing to Frieda, which somehow healed the oracle not only of her injury but age. Once she'd finished fucking us over, the oracle shoved us back out into her apartment. The rest you know."

"Your sister is the new oracle?"

I nodded.

"Hunh. It's been millennia since that's happened," he murmured thoughtfully.

"Miffed one of your champions got co-opted?"

He shook his head. "On the contrary, that explains why my reservoir of magic is stronger. When your sister took over the oracle's power, it must not have been compatible with my blessing, so it returned to me."

"You have magic again?"

"Yes, but I can't keep it." His lips turned down.

"Why not?"

"Because the moment Ariadne and I share a world again, she'll siphon it, making herself stronger."

I grimaced. "That's bullshit."

"That's part of the curse." He tapped the collar at his neck. A collar I'd ignored when I'd been taking my pleasure with his body. A body now once more clothed. Pity. I'd enjoyed exploring it in the dark and would love to see it in daylight.

"What are you going to do with the excess magic?"

"The only thing I can do. Give it away."

I arched a brow. "Going to bless a new champion?" I tried to not let any jealousy enter that query.

He snorted. "I have all the champion I need in you."

"Enyo still has your blessing too."

"But she is far away. Which means you'll have to receive the gift."

"I thought you already gave me your gift. Twice," I murmured with a wink.

Who said a god couldn't blush? "We should transfer it now before anything further happens."

"Are you sure? I mean, don't you want to keep it for a little bit?"

His lips twisted. "While I would love nothing more than to wield my own power again, I also recognize that keeping it makes it possible for Ariadne to get stronger. All it would take is her arrival in Zuzamenn and—" He snapped his fingers.

"Good point. Okay then, how do we do this?" I stepped close to him and closed my eyes before uttering, "Bless me, oh mighty monster god."

"So irreverent," he muttered before he leaned down and his mouth pressed against mine.

Mmm. A kiss. *Don't mind if I do.*

I wrapped my arms around his neck, feeling a tingling that started out familiar and carnal, then turned into a jolt of lightning. My body went stiff, my mouth parted on a gasp, and my eyes rolled back in my head. I jiggled like I'd grabbed hold of an electrical wire.

When I recovered, it was to find myself held close to Typhon.

"Well, damn," I huffed. "Getting magic never gets any easier." I glanced at him. "Which reminds me, in Bane's cave, when the portal opened and me and my sisters got struck by that lightning..."

"I'd accumulated some magic while incarcerated, and knowing Ariadne would steal it the moment I entered the world again, and sensing champions blessed in my name, I cast it out."

"Hence why we all got stronger," I mused aloud. I cast him a glance from under my lashes. "You okay with me being the powerhouse in this relationship?"

"We aren't in a relationship."

"Oh really?" My brow arched. "Not going to fuck me ever again?"

For a second, I had him stumped. His mouth opened and shut before he sighed. "I am not ready for this era."

At his reply, I laughed. "More like you'll never be ready for me, but it's okay." I tapped his cheek. "I'll drag you kicking and screaming to bed if I have to."

"There will be screaming, but only because you're climaxing," he growled.

I laughed. "I should hope so. That's my favorite part." The moment of levity faded as the reality around us penetrated once more. I sighed. "Guess we need to figure out our next move. The oracle said we had to confront the deusvenati on their turf. But my question is, how to get there?"

"We find the archway to their world."

That sounded easy enough, but I had questions. "I'm surprised they have one. I mean them being anti-magic and all, not to mention, I thought their armor absorbed magic. How is it they can use the portals at all?"

His lips flattened. "The archways aren't magical but rather permanent passages."

"Not that permanent, or hadn't you noticed how the ones on Earth were broken?"

"Think of them as a doorway, then. The arches open from one place to another, but that access can be destroyed."

"You said they can't go to Earth, though. Why?"

"I don't know." He shrugged. "I assume there is some reason, but I've never been privy to it."

"So you're only assuming they can't." I frowned. "Meaning my siblings could be in danger if the deusvenati chose to follow."

Suddenly panicked, I didn't think. I opened a shortcut between us and the arch we'd used to arrive. I emerged from my quick trip to see the door crushed, the stone edifice now rubble.

My mouth rounded. "It's broken. What if they didn't escape?" I glanced around, suddenly terrified I'd find my siblings' lifeless bodies.

Typhon, who'd followed me, knelt and put a hand on a chunk of the debris before murmuring, "The deusvenati must have gotten here before them and blocked their escape."

"Oh no. No," I wailed. I'd failed my sisters. They'd—

"Calm yourself." Typhon put a hand on my shoulder. "Your sisters aren't dead."

"How can you be so sure?"

He stared at me.

And it took me a second to realize I'd have felt it if they died. But still... "Okay, so they live. Doesn't mean they're safe."

"There are two possibilities," he stated. "One, the deusvenati captured them. Two, they escaped via another portal."

"What about the third option? They're hiding somewhere on this plane." I glanced around as if I could see them.

He snorted. "You're smarter than this."

My shoulders slumped. "If they'd remained on Zuzamenn, I'd know it. Okay, so how do we figure out where they are?"

"We can enter the available portals one by one and see if you feel them on the other side."

My nose wrinkled. "That sounds time consuming. If the deusvenati took them, that could be the difference between life and death."

He didn't argue with my statement.

I chewed the tip of my thumb. What to do? Chase after my sisters, or continue on the original quest? If my sisters were captured, then I had to save them. If they were safe in another dimension, then the best thing I could do was eliminate the threat to them.

"We need to go to the deusvenati world," I announced.

"No." He just had one word, and it took me by surprise.

"Why not? It solves a few problems at once. One, we'll find out if they have my sisters. Two, we possibly locate Ariadne."

"Too dangerous." He shook his head.

"I thought you wanted your power back?"

"I do, but even I recognize how foolhardy it

would be for the two of us to enter the deusvenati stronghold alone."

"Then how are we supposed to defeat Ariadne?" Not to mention, the oracle had said we needed to go there.

He rolled his shoulders. "I don't know. Perhaps we can't."

Such a defeatist attitude and very unlike the god I'd come to know. Which could only mean one thing. "You can't let your affection for me cloud your judgement."

"I am not—"

I cut him off. "It's not your fault. I am rather incredible. In *and* out of the sack. But the fact remains that so long as Ariadne has your stolen power, she's a threat. She needs to be handled."

"We have no way to fight the deusvenati."

"Then we don't fight them." An idea began to form in my mind. "We need to go back to town." Once more I ripped open a shortcut and returned to the devastation. I glanced around, seeking something in particular. Of all the bodies lying prone, I didn't see any in golden armor, but... I stalked to the fae woman and crouched.

"What are you doing?" he asked.

Rather than reply, I grabbed her body and

heaved it, avoiding a look at her smushed face in favor of grabbing the golden arm that was hidden under her. The one lopped off during the battle.

I hefted it with interest. And immediately dropped it.

I grimaced. "The spell-sucking magic is still active."

"Because it's not a spell." Typhon knelt and pointed. "The metal itself is what absorbs the magic."

My lips pursed. "What's it doing with it, though?"

"I don't understand."

I gestured to the armor, which retained its golden sheen despite its wearer being gone. "Power doesn't just disappear. If it's absorbing it, then it must be going somewhere." I took a second before asking, "Is this metal the same as that around your neck?"

"Possibly. Why?"

"Because your collar is linked to a matching bracelet, right?" At his nod, I added, "Therefore it stands to reason the armor is also paired to something."

"Not sure why that matters."

I didn't either, but I had to wonder what the

deusvenati were doing with all the magic they'd been accumulating.

I grimaced as I lifted the severed arm, blocking my magic from leaking. The fleshy arm suddenly slid out and flopped to the ground. I almost decorated it with barf.

"It looks human." If I ignored the blue blood stains.

"In most respects they are. Their evolutionary differences are minor."

"Have humans killed deities?" I used to think that impossible, but apparently, it was just difficult.

"From what I've been able to gather, some were killed. Others went mad and took their own lives. Some simply moved away."

"Why?" I asked as I turned over the metal casing that was doing its best to suck me dry.

"Given what I know of Earth's history, sometimes a civilization outgrows deities. Earth certainly has. I couldn't believe how few remain."

"I mean, why did the deusvenati kill theirs?"

"If rumor can be believed, a great war was waged between two gods on their world. It involved much magic and devastating results. By the time it was done, only one god remained, but the people on both sides were angry. Angry at what had been wrought in the name of power, and so they set out to rid themselves of all magic."

"How did my mom get a hold of the bracelet and collar she gave Ariadne? I can't see her going somewhere that hates gods just to help someone else with their revenge."

"Again, according to stories, the deusvenati tried to spread their gospel of god-hate to other worlds. It mostly failed, but in their effort to convert, some of the devices were left behind."

"I'm surprised they weren't destroyed."

"You shouldn't be. There will always be those wanting to use others," he said softly.

"I know you didn't want me messing with your collar while Ariadne is elsewhere with your power, but what if we went to the deusvenati world—"

"Nullarcana."

"What?"

"That's the name of their dimension."

Despite having heard him mention it once before when naming the dimensions, I snickered as the play on words caught my attention. "Wow, talk about a lack of imagination."

"Would you prefer its original name of Atlantis?"

My mouth rounded. "Fuck off. It is not." At his serious expression, I added, "Atlantis was a place on Earth."

"Earth used to have a permanent portal on an island that linked the two worlds. But the gods of our plane severed it when the deusvenati revolted and killed their god."

"Well, shit." Not much else to say because hot damn. This kept getting more interesting. "So I do have a question. If the deusvenati hate magic, why would Ariadne go there? She had to know they'd either kill or corral her."

"Can one really understand the mind of someone gone mad?"

I shook my head. "She is too crafty. She must have a reason." I eyed the golden metal left behind. "How hard would it be to create a replica of this armor?"

"Not hard but I have to ask, why?"

"Camouflage. If we're going to visit Atlantis, we need to blend in."

"That won't work. They don't have female soldiers."

"Because they're sexist. I get it. But here's the

thing. We don't have to both be soldiers." A plan began to form in my mind. "What if a soldier who got left behind suddenly returned with a prisoner?"

"They'll know I'm not one of them."

"Don't be so sure." I tugged his hand and led him up the street to where I saw another golden glint and pointed at the smashed body under a camel lizard. "They didn't collect all of their dead."

"If anyone speaks to me, they'll know right away," he pointed out.

"Then avoid talking much. Besides, they're going to be distracted by your witchy prisoner."

"Absolutely not," he exploded.

"Admit it, it's a great plan. A not-so-dead deusvenati returns with a magical prize."

"That might end up dead the moment we cross over."

"If they were killing witches on sight, why take the townspeople with power? Why not slaughter them where they found them?" I shook my head. "They captured them for a reason."

"Why are you so determined to go?"

"Because the oracle said we had to."

"Since when do you listen to anyone giving

you orders?" he grumbled. "And besides, didn't you say she claimed not all would return?"

"She did, but here's the thing. I have to go because that's the only way I can be sure my sisters aren't there. It's also the only way we can see what Ariadne's up to."

"If she's there. And even if she is, how do you expect to get close? I don't know that world. Couldn't navigate it. Even if we got lucky and landed in the right city, I would assume Ariadne, with the magic she holds, will be under heavy guard."

"I can't believe the god of monsters just wants to give up."

His jaw tensed. "I don't. But I'm also not eager to get ourselves captured or killed."

"Pessimist. Have a little faith, because here's the thing. If we get close enough to Ariadne that I can remove the controlling bracelet, you get your power back, right?"

"Yes."

"Surely an almighty monster god can control a bunch of misotheists in tin cans?"

His lips quirked. "Maybe."

"Only maybe?"

"Need I remind you they killed their last god?"

"Don't compare yourself to an idiot. Send a few big monsters after them, and that will get them rethinking their life choices. Not to mention, that god didn't have me on their side." I winked.

"It's a terrible plan."

"Got a better one?"

"No."

"Do you want to go back to Earth and mope about it until you're old?"

"I won't get old."

"You won't be a god again either without taking a risk."

He glanced at the sky and didn't say anything for a moment, so I prodded.

"Need I remind you that a certain god showed up on my doorstep demanding I help get his power back?"

"I recall. But that was before."

"Before what?"

His lips pinched. "Nothing. Very well. You want to try this foolhardy plan, then how's this?"

His flowing cloak suddenly sucked into his body and changed, molding to his frame, becoming golden armor that encased him head to toe.

I whistled at the end result. "Damn. You look just like one of those bastards."

"You, however, are lacking something." His voice had a tinny sound to it. He held out his hand and, on it, formed a circlet of dull metal just like the one he wore.

I gulped. "Is that—"

"A fake. Thank my cloak for agreeing to part with a tiny bit of itself to complete the disguise." He held it out to me, and I hesitated before grabbing it.

Knowing it wasn't real didn't ease the trepidation of putting it around my neck, feeling the choking solidness of it. For a moment I panicked when it sealed shut.

Typhon grabbed me by the arms and soothed, "Fear not, you still have your magic."

It took me sending out a blast and punching a hole through a wall to sigh in relief. "Sorry."

"Don't be. I well remember how it felt when mine went on and I was suddenly cut off from everything."

"Were you always a god?" I asked suddenly.

"No. Gods are made, not born."

"Made how?"

"Through extraordinary circumstances."

I smelled a story, but it would have to wait because, with our disguises in place, there was only one thing left to do.

I dragged him into the empty bakery where death hadn't struck and fucked him. Fucked a god until he bellowed my name.

# 15

## Typhon

Typhon didn't like the plan. Not one bit. Even though it was actually quite clever.

Camouflaged as one of the deusvenati, while stomach churning, would give him the ability to move around Nullarcana. Or, as Deino preferred to call it, Atlantis.

The part he disliked? Putting Deino in danger.

Seeing that collar around her neck filled him with fear, a fear that it would be replaced with the real version. That she would become a slave—or worse—to his quest.

If someone had told him he would one day wonder if vengeance and a return to power were truly necessary, he would have taken their head. But now... Now he'd found a measure of happiness with this woman. Discovered something worth protecting. Someone to love.

*Ack.*

She must have cast a spell on him. The god of monsters didn't love. He couldn't. The beasts he prevailed over would have eaten him up and spit out his bones if he were so soft, yet there was no denying the affection he had for her.

But could he tell her that?

No.

Could he forbid her from doing this?

No.

He could only hope they prevailed, because anything else? Unacceptable.

"So where is the portal for Atlantis?" she asked.

"Right there." He indicated the arm that had flopped to the ground.

She glanced at it. "I don't see any directions."

"It has none, but its owner originated in Atlantis, meaning you can use it as a focal point to see where it came from."

Her lips pursed. "I've never done that."

"In that case, let's go home."

Her nose wrinkled. "I have no home, remember? The monsters destroyed it, and those fuckers will keep coming after me and my siblings until Ariadne is stopped. I have to figure this out so we can find that twat, cut off her head, and get you back in power. The sooner the better."

"Cut off her head?" he questioned.

"I've seen too many movies where the bad guy gets back up after the hero thinks he's dealt a death wound to take chances."

"I think I need to watch more of these movies. In my time, dead people didn't rise unless a necromancer commanded them to."

"You and I are going to have some epic couch snuggles when this is over. But first..." She squatted and squinted at the arm. "How do I make it into a compass?"

"You need to scry its movements." He explained the process, and with a look of concentration, Deino cast the spell on the arm, which jerked.

Startled, she fell from her haunches to her butt. "It moved."

"How else is it supposed to guide?" was his dry retort.

She glared. "You could have warned me."

He shrugged. "Now you know."

"Um, is it going to claw its way there?"

"Not without a lot of effort. You'll have to pick it up to follow the path it took."

"Pick it up? Ew. No. You do it."

"The magic will work better if the caster is the one making the connection."

"This sucks," she complained, but she still bent down and grabbed the arm. She held it out in front of her with a grimace. "This way," she stated as she began to walk.

They weaved through the small town, a place that didn't deserve the tragedy visited upon it. A place that he could have saved had he been full power.

Deino wasn't the only one dealing with guilt. He'd hoped the deusvenati would leave when they realized all the magical targets had fled, but instead, they'd turned murderous.

Why? Not a question he'd often asked himself. As the god of monsters, senseless violence was something he'd gotten used to. Before, at any rate. Then he lived in solitude and emerged with a better appreciation for life.

As they reached the edge of the town, Deino

paused to look back. "It feels wrong to leave those bodies unburied.

"Burial is a very Earth thing. In other civilizations, cremation is preferred as it's thought to release the spirit after death."

"And we're sure there's no one living left behind, maybe hiding?"

He shook his head. "They were thorough."

"In that case…" She swept her hand through the air, and the air crackled with power, heating and whipping around her until she flung it. A wave of fire spread outward, the flame of it blue and white, the most intense they could get. Hot enough to cleanse.

She turned her back on the inferno she used to sweep the town clean and marched toward the wasteland and the archway they could see in the distance.

Unlike the one for Earth, warnings were posted around it: *Danger.* He had to wonder why it had never been destroyed. If all the portals to Atlantis had been broken, the deusvenati would have been stuck.

Perhaps if they did succeed, he would make it his mission to ensure all the doorways were closed.

*If* they succeeded…

The odds weren't in their favor. Two of them against all of the forces in Atlantis. This was foolish. They'd be killed before they ever got close to Ariadne.

As they neared the portal, he shed all doubt.

Doubt was for mortals.

Trepidation for the cowardly.

Head held high, he stood by his witch's side and murmured, "Are you ready?"

"If I said no—"

"I'd whisk you away."

She glanced at him. "You'd give up your godhood for me?"

A good thing she couldn't see his face as he lied, "You're no use to me dead."

"As if I'm going to die. My sister told me I have a great destiny." She stood by the edge of the portal and held out her hand. "Coming, oh mighty captor?"

He stood before the archway, a stony maw that would shortly swallow them whole. A terrible analogy given his trepidation over the quest. A qualm not shared by his bold witch.

"I'll do my best to remain by your side," he promised as they stepped into the portal.

They went from a barren wasteland to a cave

of tan-colored stone, which appeared to be home to thirteen portals, only three of them still intact. Not surprising, given the actions of the deusvenati.

A golden-armored soldier snoozed against a wall, snoring behind his helm. Typhon held his finger to his lips, thinking it best they sneaked past, but his witch had other plans.

"Let me go, you brute." She shoved away from him and fled across the room, waking the sleeping soldier, who jumped to his feet.

"Halt. Who goes there?"

"Golden devils! How dare you take me hostage!" Deino snapped, looking utterly crazed.

"Where did you come from?" the soldier demanded.

That was Typhon's cue. "Zuzamenn. I've returned with a captive."

"I thought all troops returned yesterday." The fellow sounded puzzled.

"I got trapped in a building with this witch." He tried to add a sneer to his tone. "She fought me, but I prevailed. I've brought her back to face judgement." He did his best to improvise, and to his surprise, it worked.

"The Enclave will be pleased. We lost too

many in that attack, and they returned with only two others weak in the source."

"Was the oracle one of them?" he fished, seeing how Deino's eyes widened, probably wondering if they were her sisters.

The fellow shook his head. "Minor witches barely worth collaring."

"Take off this slave ring and I'll show you a real witch," hissed Deino, really playing up her role.

"Feisty," commented the soldier.

"You have no idea," Typhon's replied dryly. "I'll take her to her new home."

The soldier snickered. "She won't be cocky for long."

Typhon gripped her by the arm and marched her out of the only open doorway, keeping quiet until they were in a narrow stone hallway.

"Can you feel your sisters?" he whispered.

She shook her head. "Nope. What about you? Is Ariadne here?"

He nodded. He'd felt the difference the moment he crossed over, the tug at his essence. And if he felt her, chances were she felt him too. "We'll have to move quickly before she notifies the deusvenati."

"Can you use your connection to find her?"

He shook his head. "Oddly enough, no. It's not like the bond you have with your sisters. It was why I needed help on Earth locating her fortress."

The tunnel they traversed spilled into a large chamber with several tunnels branching off it and a row of five golden guards.

"I've brought back a witch for the enclave," he stated upon seeing them.

"We'll take her from here," declared the one holding a spear.

Typhon readied to argue, when Deino sprang into action. "You'll never put me in a cell." She ran, bolting past them to the doorway on the left. The armored soldiers looked at each other as if having a silent argument.

"I guess I'll go get her," he offered when none of them moved.

"Better you than me," mumbled the guy with the spear.

He wondered at their reluctance and if he'd blown his cover by offering to fetch the fleeing witch. But he'd promised to stay close by, and so he shadowed her steps in the tunnel that crept upwards, the air getting hotter with each stride.

Dusty too. By the time he found Deino, she was standing still at a doorway she'd tugged partially open.

She glanced at him. "Stay away from me!"

"It's me," he murmured.

"Just making sure."

"Why did you run?"

"Because something told me to come this way." She turned to look back through the door. "I don't think the deusvenati live on the surface."

"What makes you think that?"

She shoved the door wide so he could see. Or not see. He could tell he looked outside only because of the nimbus of the sun barely visible for the dirt whipping around.

He stepped past the threshold to get a proper glimpse and was struck by the devastation. When the winds died down for a moment, and an area of dust settled, he could see the remnants of a city, partially buried in dunes, eroded, and in places falling down. No hint of life, not even a single tree or hardy bush. The dry heat tightened his lungs enough he coughed.

He went back inside, and she shut the door.

"Their world is dead," she declared.

He coughed again. "The air is polluted."

"I know. I had to put on a magic mask halfway up the tunnel. What do you think happened? It's like a nuke went off."

"What is a nuke?"

"Giant bomb that wipes out everything, while poisoning the land and air for centuries."

"Humans created that?" At her nod, he exclaimed, "Why?"

"Because we're violent. But I don't get the impression these guys are into technology so I'm thinking maybe a volcano erupted and fucked the environment. Or maybe an asteroid hit."

"It's because their god died."

She blinked at him. "How is that possible? A bunch of Earth's gods are dead and gone and we're not a wasteland."

"Some places are more reliant on gods than others. And Earth still has many left. In this case, the planet was likely not viable until a deity took interest and made it habitable."

"So the deusvenati fucked themselves when they killed him."

"Yes."

"If that's the case, why are they such assholes about getting rid of magic elsewhere?"

"I don't know. Like I don't know why they appear to be collecting people with magic."

"Guess we'll have to go back down and find out." Her nose wrinkled. "Dammit. I was hoping to explore a bit more before getting shoved in a cage. Oh well, at least I still have my magic."

"Be sure to not let them see. They must believe you are nullified."

"I know. Don't worry. Let's go before they come looking."

Not something they needed to worry about, as they encountered no one on their way down, which led to him slowing his step before the chamber, murmuring, "Something isn't right."

"We can't turn back now," she stated before stepping boldly into the room with the guards.

He was only a second behind her. A second too late to stop her from being grabbed and a real collar being closed around her throat. During that second of shock, he couldn't avoid his own capture. A net of the magic-numbing metal dropped over him, making it impossible to fight.

Impossible to do anything as the deusvenati took Deino away.

And dropped him down a deep hole.

# 16

So I might have been a tad too cocky. My plan was not well thought out. My prospects looked dim. I didn't realize how much I'd relied on my magic until it disappeared.

The most annoying part? I never even had a chance to try and use my magic before a ring came around my neck, choking off my ability. I almost sobbed as I became mundane for the first time since I got my powers at sixteen.

Rescue seemed unlikely. Poor Typhon found himself just as badly trapped, the net they flung over him turning his golden armor into a dull cloak that hung limp without a single smoky ripple.

Fuck.

I glared at the golden knights. "Unhand me at once. I am a citizen of Earth." Probably the dumbest thing I could have said.

And yet they didn't laugh, just grabbed me roughly, a soldier on each side with a tight grip on my arms as they dragged me into a tunnel. I didn't bother fighting as they carried me off to a cell. Better preserve my strength for a proper escape. Remaining calm meant I could observe and catalogue. I counted the left and right turns as they trotted me through tunnels hewn into rock. Took note of the fetid stench of people living without fresh air. The gaunt faces that peeked out at times from crevices we passed. Abject poverty and misery hung thickly in the air along with despair.

What a horrible place. The deusvenati were a people moving toward extinction, so I had to wonder why they were so aggressive. You'd think they'd be looking to make alliances. Or at the very least relocating. Yet their destruction of Zuzamenn showed they had another plan in mind. One that didn't involve taking over the town for the poor people I saw. A plan that had them kidnapping those with magic.

What did they have planned for me? Nothing

good, I imagined. I couldn't help but remember the oracle's words that a mortal wouldn't return. Me, I was that mortal.

Fuck.

We entered a tunnel lined with veritable dungeon cells. I got tossed into an empty one comprised of three walls of stone, the fourth facing the corridor being simply bars embedded in rock. No window. Then again, I'd seen the outside. Wasn't a great view. Wouldn't recommend. Zero stars.

"What's going to happen to me?" I asked as I scrambled to my feet before the door to my cell clanged shut.

No reply. The guards remained silent as they stomped off. Once the echo of their steps faded, I realized I wasn't alone. Someone sobbed nearby.

I grabbed the bars and did my best to peek. "Hello? Anyone here?" I called out.

"I'm here," said a low voice from across the hall. A huddled figure, whose rags had helped them blend into the rock, rose to their feet.

"Who are you? I'm Dina. From Earth." I introduced myself first.

"Barabella, from Zuzamenn," murmured the woman who cautiously approached the bars of her prison.

Rather than ask her about the recent fight, I went straight to the point. "Do you know what the deusvenati want with us?"

"Death!" screamed another woman, the same one who'd been sobbing. "We will all die."

"Yeah, I'd rather not," was my retort which caused Barabella to snort.

"Ignore Lacie. She's always been very dramatic."

"Well, she's got reason this time. Situation doesn't look good," I conceded.

"No. It's not. But where there's life, there's hope," Barabella said serenely.

I liked her attitude. "Have you spoken to anyone since your arrival? Any clue as to why they've taken us?"

Barabella, who'd joined me at her set of bars, shook her head. "No one will speak to me. The soldiers only came by once before they brought you to fetch the previous occupant of your cell."

Taking a wild guess, I said, "A witch?"

"Dwarven wizard. Before he was taken away, we spoke. He claimed to be the last of eight taken from his world."

Eight and none of them returned. Really not a

good sign. "And no idea what they're doing with them, hunh?"

"No. But I have a theory," she whispered.

"What is it?"

"They are sacrificing us in the hopes of appeasing their god."

"I thought they killed their god."

Barabella's lips turned down. "Whatever the case, I believe they've come to regret what they did."

Thinking of what I'd seen topside, I kind of agreed. "Without a necromancer, I don't think they stand a chance in reviving a dead god."

The comment led to Barabella shrugging. "I don't know what will or won't work, but I do hope if their god returns, he smites them all for being twats."

A woman after my own heart.

We spoke a little after that, with her asking me where I came from. I told her about Earth. I omitted the part about being there when Zuzamenn fell. She had enough to deal with as it was, and I still felt guilty. I didn't need the only person talking to me getting pissy because I hadn't done more to save her and the town.

Time passed, how much I couldn't tell. I

could say, however, that the collar wasn't coming off no matter how much I tugged or cursed at it. Nor could I feel my magic, not one bit. Adding to my annoyance, I missed Typhon.

Was he okay? Injured? Dead... I'd like to think that given I carried some of his power inside me I'd know if he'd been obliterated.

When company arrived, we knew in advance by the clomping of the boots. The golden guards arrived and halted between my and Barabella's cells. Both of our doors were opened.

The guard that grabbed my arm got his gauntlet slapped.

"I can walk. No need to manhandle," I snapped in my haughtiest tone.

While I presented a brave font, Barabella wailed and clung at her bars, her seeming calm nonchalance of before just a front. We got marched—well I did, Barabella got dragged—through the network of tunnels, completely wrecking my memorization of before. I'd never find my way back to the room with the portal without a guide.

The soldiers marched us into a massive cave, the ceiling of it soaring high enough I didn't feel

## Gentleman and the Witch

claustrophobic. The air appeared fresher here, and yet I saw no sign of a ventilation system.

In this space milled people without armor. Women and children bedraggled and thin, their hollow cheeks a sign of scarce food. Their pallor resulted from the lack of natural light. Of interest, not a single man was without the golden armor.

The person who drew the eye, though, currently sat on a throne carved out of bone, the long teeth of the massive creature making me glad I didn't have to face it.

I recognized the woman reigning over the cavern, a voluptuous beauty with a perpetual bitch face that went well with her ostentatious crown. Ariadne wore white as if that would purify her evil intentions.

"I should have known the tin suits were acting on the orders of a thieving cunt." I didn't bother with politeness.

"You are a mouthy one. And stupid too. Thinking you and Typhon could waltz into my kingdom. As if I wouldn't know the moment you stepped out of the portal. My army might not have seen through your disguise, but you can't fool me." Ariadne smirked.

"Speaking of disguise, do your tin soldiers

know you're a glorified witch?" I glanced at the guards flanking me. "You might want to collar the cunt on the throne. She's a liar and a thief and has way more magic than me."

Laughter burst out of Ariadne. "Nice try, but the deusvenati know exactly who and what I am. Who do you think placed me on their throne?"

The news surprised, and I couldn't hide it.

"I can see you're confused, but it's actually quite simple. The deusvenati are an interesting people. They destroyed their god to free themselves from tyranny, only to find themselves worse off because they had no idea their god had been using his magic to make this world habitable. The descent began slowly, the skies turning dark with dust, which led to their crops failing and the water fouling. Within a few generations, they moved underground, where they learned how to farm mushrooms and lichen to survive. But now even that is failing. The deusvenati are dying, soon to be no more."

"They'd be fine if they relocated," I pointed out.

"Some have, but most would rather see their planet return to its former glory."

"What does this have to do with putting your psycho ass on a throne?" I questioned.

"They've realized they need magic to return."

"And so, what? They're kidnapping wizards and witches in the hopes having them around will somehow fix their world?" I kept her talking because the more she yapped, the more I learned. The more I learned, the better my chance for survival. Or so I told myself.

"Oh, we don't keep them for long. After all, the deusvenati don't need extra mouths to feed."

"You're killing them." Stated, not asked.

Her teeth gleamed as she said, "Yes."

"Isn't that counterintuitive? I mean if you're trying to bring back magic, then how does killing them help since their power dies with them?"

"Not if sacrificed correctly. See, when their god died, the reservoir of magic it maintained, the source that kept their planet from collapsing, dried up. With my help, they've been filling it."

I arched a brow. "Doesn't seem to be working. In case you didn't notice, the planet is still a shithole."

"Because we've only been able to donate small amounts thus far. But having you here will change that."

Not the most promising thing to hear. "How come they haven't sacrificed you? After all, you've got tons of magic." I glanced at the soldier flanking me and admitted in an aside, "She stole a god's powers."

Ariadne chuckled. "They already know. The first thing I did upon encountering them was prove I could do miracles." She waved her hand and drew my attention to a lush garden area on the other side of her throne.

"You grew plants?"

"Creation and life are the purview of gods. And as a god, I told them what they had to do if they wanted to revive their world. Under my guidance, they've been hunting down magic users and bringing them back to refill the reservoir."

"You're murdering people."

"No one that matters. And their deaths are for a greater cause. I will return Atlantis to its former glory."

I snorted. "Bullshit. You're a con artist. Do they know your cowardly ass scrammed away from Earth because you were scared of me and my sisters?"

Her jaw tensed. "I wasn't afraid."

"Yet you fled like a rat from a sinking ship," I taunted.

"And will return stronger than before. A few more sacrifices of worth and the reservoir will have enough power that I won't need Typhon. I will become a goddess in truth. More powerful than your little monster god. More powerful than anyone. All who stand in my way shall be vanquished." She stood from her throne as she announced it, and her tin cans rattled their spears.

"Nice villain speech. Now how about a reality check. The other gods aren't going to let you waltz in and cause trouble."

"Those who don't bow will face my army."

"What army? I see a few dozen people," I taunted.

Her expression twisted. "I've heard enough from you. You think you can twist my subjects against me, but they know I am their only hope."

"You're going to get them all killed," was my blunt reply. "You should be encouraging them to evacuate and find a new place to live."

"I've had enough of your poisonous tongue." She pointed. "Take her to the well! Bring all of them."

Rough grips took hold of me on either side

and dragged me toward a fancy arch, past the wilting garden. Seems Ariadne didn't have a green thumb after all.

As we entered a chamber, bare but for a well with a raised ledge, I was struck by the beauty. Unlike the network of tunnels, this room had been smoothed and polished, the stone a light tan, carved with symbols. Symbols like the ones on my back.

A place of power.

A place of magic.

A place of death.

For a second, I'd have sworn I could hear the screams of those who'd given their lives for Ariadne's mad scheme.

Oh wait, those were the screams of the living. Barabella was being held by two soldiers, and she thrashed and wailed. I couldn't blame her. No one wanted to know ahead of time they were going to die.

She glanced at me and screamed, "Do something."

Do what? I remained as powerless as her.

To my surprise, as they brought Barabella to the edge of the well, Ariadne approached and laid her fingers on the collar around the captive woman's neck. The collar opened and was grabbed.

For a second, Barabella's eyes glowed as she summoned her magic.

Then she was gone. Shoved into the hole at her feet, the noise of her scream receding until it abruptly ceased.

A shiver went down my spine. I'd yet to think of a way out of this.

I expected my turn next, but Ariadne was serious when she said she wanted to toss everyone in the well. The woman I'd heard sobbing was brought next. She didn't even try to use her power before getting shoved into the hole.

To my surprise, they had more prisoners, not all of them human appearing. One by one they got tossed. Most screamed. But one—a squat, green fellow who could have been Yoda's cousin—glared at Ariadne before jumping in of his own volition.

I doubted I could be as brave.

The line of sacrifices diminished until only I remained. My only relief was that Typhon hadn't been one of those brought forward.

Ariadne turned and smiled in my direction. "Your turn."

"My sisters will avenge me," I threatened.

"You mean they'll try. I'm expecting them to show up, and when they do..." Ariadne glanced at the well. "They should provide enough power to finally fill the reservoir and I shall ascend."

"You're insane," I muttered.

"Am I?"

The soldiers gripping me began to drag me to the edge, and my breathing quickened. I wanted to be brave. I also wanted to live.

All too quickly, I stared into the deep hole—a hole that seemed to have no end. I felt no tingling of magic. Saw no glow either. It led to me blurting out, "I don't think your reservoir is working as expected."

"It will. The oracle told me so."

I blinked. "You spoke to her? I thought she turned you away."

"She turned me away the second time I visited. But my first meeting with her was before we met. At the time, she didn't make sense. She told me I'd never get what I wanted on Earth. That I needed to go to a place where there was no god and that I would get what I deserved once I threw the monster god's champion into the well."

"That bitch!" I huffed.

"She is slippery," Ariadne agreed. "Hence why I wanted to speak with her again, but she evaded my soldiers. Pity, her magic would have been a potent addition."

"The oracle is gone." I didn't mention she passed on her mantle.

"A shame, but I have what I need in you. Any last words?"

"I hope you die painfully." I then sent a quick prayer to the only god who might be listening. *Bye, Reaper. It was nice knowing you.*

# 17

## Typhon

THE IGNOBLE CAPTURE BY THE deusvenati—using a net, of all things!—left Typhon disgruntled, but his true anger came from seeing his witch collared.

How dare they lay hands on her.

How dare they try and quell the spark within her.

But worst of all, what would they do to Deino?

He didn't know, and it bothered him. Roused his guilt because he knew they shouldn't have come. The plan was flawed. They needed more than a disguise. They needed an army. But she'd insisted they had to come, and like a moron who listened to his dick, he'd agreed.

And now they were both, as the modern humans would say, fucked.

As the deusvenati escorted Typhon through the rough tunnels, he couldn't help but notice the starkness of the place. How far they had fallen.

He'd known Atlantis before, when it still had magic and its pair of gods. A beautiful paradise that favored intellect and innovation over violence and strife. But then the deities that ruled it, closer than any brothers, fought. Not over land or power, but a lover.

War was waged. Devastation ensued. One god died, and the other emerged victorious, only to find out he'd actually lost because the reason for their fight fled into the arms of another.

Despondent, the remaining god didn't fix the chaos he'd wrought but rather sank into despondency. Perhaps if he'd at least mended what he'd done, the Atlanteans wouldn't have revolted. But the renamed deusvenati avenged themselves, murdering their god and, in doing so, spelled their end. An end that had just begun when Typhon had been locked away.

Judging by what he'd seen, it wouldn't be long

before they ceased to exist, which made their recent violence puzzling. Why were they still focused on eradicating magic? It made no sense.

The net, with him still in it, got tossed into a pit. The sides of it were lined in metal ore, the same sapping version that the soldiers wore. Shrugging off the netting didn't do anything to help. His cloak remained limp and dull. His senses were reduced to sight, sound, and smell.

Just like his last prison.

*The shove into the portal led to him losing his balance and stumbling as he arrived in a dark and rocky place. He fell, and it hurt! The surprise had him cursing in four different languages before he rose and dusted himself off. His cloak rippled but did nothing to stop the shiver of cold as he looked around.*

*Where am I?*

*Didn't matter. He wasn't staying. He turned to eye the place he'd emerged and noticed a column of stone carved with symbols of power but currently inert. He slapped his hand on it.*

*Nothing. Just solid stone. It probably needed an infusion of magic. He grabbed for his power, only to find it greatly weakened.*

*His fingers went to the collar around his neck,*

snapped in place when Ariadne ambushed him. He tugged. It didn't separate.

"Argh." He pulled and only managed to bruise his flesh. The collar wasn't coming off, and he'd bet it was why he had no power.

"I will kill you!" Soon as he got back to Earth.

Since he had barely a spark to call upon, he wondered how to activate the portal. The ones he usually used just required him to step through.

In this case, he bounced off the pillar and frowned. He kept frowning as he read the inscription on the column of stone, the gist of it being the door would only open when the planets aligned. He assumed that would happen at least once a day, so despite there being nothing of comfort or interest in the rocky bowl he found himself in, he remained sitting by the column. Napping out of boredom. Plotting his revenge against the woman who'd dared to steal from him.

The darkness turned to day. An orange sun rose to cast a fiery glow upon this strange world. A barren place of rocks, stunted trees, and monsters.

The first one he encountered almost took his life. It dove from the sky, talons outstretched, only its caw of hunting triumph giving him warning. He half-turned and grabbed the claws, yanking down the bird with its three eyes and a beak that snapped angrily. He narrowly avoided its chomp by shoving its head against a rock. The angry bird sheared the stone with a single bite.

A good thing it wasn't any of his body parts.

He killed it by wringing its neck and, from that point on, became more wary and savvy. He had no weapons, and so he had to create some using gnarled branches to which he attached the sharp claws. He used the bird's own beak to cut it open and gut it. A god might be immortal in the sense he wouldn't die of old age, but a lack of food would weaken him, and he could be killed.

He built a shelter by the pillar, piling rocks to create a cairn to sleep in at night. He explored the area around it and found a stream, the water metallic tasting. He kept track of the days by marking a line for each rise of the sun. At one hundred and forty-seven, while skinning a hoglike beast, the sun went dark as a moon passed over it.

In that sudden somberness, a glow startled him.

The column showed a seam!

He jumped to his feet and ran for it. At last, the door opened. He shoved his fingers into the crack and felt a resistance on the other side. A force shoved him back and he could only stare in disbelief—and a bit of horror—as his chance to escape disappeared.

The count started over.

A hundred and forty-seven days later, he stood by the column as the moon once more passed the sun.

Again, the crack never widened enough to allow him passage.

Year after year passed.

He left his camp for a time, thinking to explore the world and find another exit. He found nothing but danger and the ruins of a city long abandoned. A vast, stormy ocean thwarted his attempts to explore any other islands or continents.

When he tired of searching, he returned to the rocky valley with the pillar. When despondency made him desperate, he thought of his revenge. He couldn't die, not while Ariadne lived.

A decade passed.

Then another.

The god of monsters, once worshipped and showered with attention and gifts, became a hermit who did nothing but hunt and survive.

When the eclipse hit every one hundred and forty-seven days, he barely roused himself. He'd glance at the column, see the tiny seam and grunt.

*Therefore, when it did finally open fully, he spent a moment staring, not daring to believe.*

Move, you idiot!

*He'd walked through that doorway and found that not only had he changed but so had the world. Time had passed much more quickly than he'd realized. His century on the other side was more than a millennium on Earth. But at least he was finally free.*

However, the revenge he sought didn't come easily.

*Will I ever regain what I lost?*

He'd not lapsed into that memory to flagellate himself over his failures but to remind himself that he'd not given up when banished to that barren wasteland. He certainly wouldn't surrender hope now, not with Ariadne so close. Not with his witch in danger.

He eyed the sides of the pit, the metal and rock jagged but not enough to grip and climb. At a depth of a dozen or so feet, he couldn't jump and catch the lip either. As for tools... He didn't even have a blade, just the woven metal net.

It led to him eyeing it. He tugged at its strands. The magic-nullifying metal woven into the threads made it sturdy enough it didn't break.

A glance upward didn't show anything protruding from the lip of the pit that he could have tossed the net on.

Stumped, he sat down and meditated. As his mind relaxed, it went back to his time in his prison...

*The attack took him by surprise. The water rushing over the rocks hid the noise of the beast's advance. The slam of a heavy body pushed him to the ground, and only his honed reflexes kept him from getting chomped. He managed to slide out and roll, bouncing to his feet to see an ugly creature similar to a wolf but with leathery skin. It advanced on him, growling.*

*So he growled back. To no effect, he should add.*

*The beast leaped, and he held up his spear just in time to impale it, but the death throes snapped his weapon. He had more back at his camp, only, as he whirled to head for it, he noticed two more of the creatures waiting for him.*

*They charged at him in tandem and slammed him to the ground. He could barely hold their snapping muzzles from his flesh. If he had his godly power, he would have commanded them, but he had little magic.*

*Little and yet he had to do something, or they would tear him to shreds.*

*With nothing to lose, he huffed a word of power, pushing what little bit of magic he still had into it.* I command thee.

*One of the creatures suddenly stilled before tearing into the other one. He didn't stay to watch the outcome but hurried to his camp, lightheaded and weak.*

*But alive.*

Typhon snapped upright in the pit with a sudden idea. These caves surely had creatures roaming them, and while they might not be classed as monsters, they couldn't ignore if he pushed just right.

Given he wouldn't get more than one opportunity—because Ariadne would most likely notice—he had to make his attempt count. He listened for the scratch of claws on stone or the swish of a tail. Instead, he heard a clank as a golden figure peeked over the edge.

A monster if he'd ever seen one.

Worth a try. He threw the powerful compulsion at the soldier. *I command thee.* He threw everything he had because this would be his only chance.

## Gentleman and the Witch

The soldier froze before he extended a hand. Typhon quickly tossed the netting high enough the gauntleted fingers caught and held it. He clambered up the side of the pit, moving fast lest the order wear off and he plummet. At the top, he didn't pause before grabbing the helmet and twisting. He had no doubt the soldier would have attacked the moment the magic wore off.

The body fell to his feet, limp, and Typhon stripped it of its sword before he dumped the body in the pit. He grimaced as the pommel tried to suck his power. It rendered his cloak inert, but he'd spent a century honing his body. His strength came from hard work. His speed from practice. His determination was fueled by vengeance.

He glanced around. The room had only a single light, some kind of glowing rock, barely enough to illuminate. He saw nothing of interest, just a single exit.

The corridor beyond was also empty, and he knew from recollection of the memorized path how to get back to the portal room. A selfish god who'd just escaped a long isolation could have returned to that chamber and chosen to leave, but Typhon was more than a god. He was also a man and a lover with a score to settle—and a witch to save. Arrogance and anger fueled his brisk stride.

He encountered no one in his path, not that it would have mattered. He simmered and boiled, ready to fight. If he died, so be it. He tired of cowering.

Finding his witch didn't take much effort. She was connected to him by more than his blessing. The moments they'd shared had entwined them in a way he wasn't yet ready to define. It surprised him to find the tunnels so empty. Then again, would a dying world really have that many people left? How many had been sacrificed in their razing of Zuzamenn? And why?

The connection he had to his witch grew strong, and he knew he'd find her at the end of the hall. He strode into the chamber, only to halt suddenly at the sight.

Firstly, there was Ariadne with a smug smile of triumph, wearing a crown, thinking she'd already won.

Second, he'd found his witch, looking beautiful and unafraid as she stood on the edge of an abyss.

But the most shocking thing of all in this room? The power boiling below their feet.

"What have you done?" he accused.

"You! How did you escape?" Ariadne's eyes narrowed in anger.

"I asked, what have you done?" His voice reverberated, causing a slight tremor in the rock.

Whimpers drew his glance to the people gathered and huddled by the walls. So few, and frightened. They should be. A bomb brewed under their feet.

"She's been killing arcane users and storing their magic in the well," Deino shouted. "She thinks she can use it to become a real goddess."

"Are you mad?" he breathed.

Ariadne pursed her lips. "Hardly. We both know gods are made. Speaking of which, any last words before you die and your power becomes mine?"

"Kill me and you'll be next." He dropped to his haunches, put his hand on the floor, and felt the tremor of power in need of an outlet.

"What are you doing?" Ariadne snapped.

His lips twisted. "Seeing how long we have before your arrogance destroys this planet."

"Shut your lying mouth. I know what I'm doing."

"No, you don't. Otherwise, you'd know you

can't mix powers. My power and what's brewing in that well are incompatible." There was a reason why gods couldn't just murder each other to get stronger.

"You're just saying that because you're jealous I'm going to be more formidable than you ever could be." Ariadne refused to listen.

"I'm saying it because I'd rather not die when you destroy this planet with your stupidity," he spat.

"You're lying. I've had the power of three gods without issue."

"Via the collars and their matching bands. But the power was never truly yours. Remove the band and"—he snapped his fingers—"you'll be mundane again."

"He's telling the truth." Deino jumped into the conversation. "When Frieda was gifted the oracle's power, she lost her blessing from Typhon."

The news narrowed Ariadne's gaze. "Your sister is the oracle? Good to know."

"Not really. She's the one who told me to come here and stop you. You're going to fail," Deino stated.

Doubt entered Ariadne's expression, and while she mulled over the news, Typhon glanced at Deino still on the edge of the pit. He had to get her away from here before the worst happened.

"You seem awfully concerned with the witch," Ariadne stated, noticing his attention had wavered.

"She's my champion."

"I think she's more than that." Ariadne waved a hand. "Enough blathering. Toss her in!"

"No!" he roared as he surged into action.

"Seize him!" Ariadne shouted.

Her soldiers tried. The first two died. He slashed and stabbed with the sword he'd stolen, but their sheer numbers overwhelmed. He found himself crushed under their weight, pinned to the floor.

Deino screamed, "Leave him alone, you twat! Haven't you done enough to him?"

Ariadne moved to stand over him, looking smug as she knelt to brush her fingers over the collar at his throat. "Your champion defends you staunchly even as she stands on the eve of her death, and now I wonder, do I make you watch her die, or should her last memory be that of you being torn apart by my soldiers?"

In the grips of her golden defenders, Typhon seethed, too impotent to do anything.

"Or do I throw you in the well?" Ariadne mused aloud.

"Do it," he dared. "It will strip me of my power, and you will return to being just Ariadne the mortal with no magic to keep you young. Not that it will matter, as that will be the match to light the bomb you've created."

A perturbed Ariadne retreated from him. "Your lies bore me. This conversation is done, and lucky for you, I won't kill you. I'm going to let you live. Live with the knowledge your champion has failed. Live knowing I've become greater than you could imagine." She snapped her fingers. "Take him to the third portal and toss him in. Once you do, shatter it so he can't return."

As the soldiers dragged Typhon away, he fought, but their armor sapped his magic, and their sheer numbers overwhelmed his skill and strength. There was no escape.

The deusvenati brought him to the portal chamber, and he struggled in their grip. He couldn't leave. Not with Deino literally on the precipice of danger. He had to save her.

The portal loomed, and he eyed it, wondering where it would send him.

The moment he hit the rocks on the other side he knew.
No.
Not again.
He was back in his prison.

# 18

Poor Typhon. He'd been so brave coming to my rescue. For a second, I thought he'd even convinced Ariadne to not go through with her nutty plan. But the twat was strong in her, and so she had her bullies gang up on Typhon, taking him away, sending him who knew where, but at least he lived.

The prognosis on my fate? Not so good.

*A mortal won't return.*

The oracle had predicted my death—the original oracle, at any rate. My own sister never said anything. On the contrary, she'd made it sound like me coming here was our best and only shot.

Had Frieda seen me die? It seemed odd she'd not warned me.

"Well, now that we've handled that interruption, shall we?" Ariadne stated.

"In a second. Where did you send him?" I couldn't stem my curiosity.

"A place he knows very well. A place with no escape, at least not until the next eclipse."

It took me a single, horrified blink to decipher her claim. "You put him back in his prison?"

"Turns out there was an available exit the entire time. Who knew Atlantis had a permanent doorway? Guess he never found it. And by the time the next positioning rolls around again on Earth, you'll be long gone, and I will be a goddess." She cackled.

"What is wrong with you?" I yelled. "Haven't you punished him enough? And for what? The fact you were miserable in your marriage? Did it never occur to you to get a divorce?"

"You know nothing," hissed Ariadne. "In my day, women had no power. We were simply chattel relying on men for a home, clothing, and food. Marriage wasn't a choice."

"Being unhappy isn't an excuse for torturing someone," I countered.

"I'd hardly call exile torture," she replied coyly.

"How did you get the extra collars?" I asked.

"After your mother gave me the first set, I went looking and found a few more in a bazaar in a dimension with no magic at all. I returned a few times looking for more, but alas, deusvenati artifacts aren't exactly prized."

I glanced at the golden tin cans standing sentinel. "I can't believe they can listen to you and not realize you're a fraud."

"Hardly a fraud. They've been waiting for me. Apparently, before they killed their last seer, a prophecy was uttered. It said that a woman from the forbidden planet, wielding the might of the monster god, would be their salvation and bring about the return of magic and glory."

It was obvious Ariadne thought it referred to her, so I smirked and tossed a match into her oily logic. "Who says it's talking about you? After all, I am from Earth, the forbidden world. I also have the true blessing of the monster god and not the stolen magic. Who's to say I'm not the salvation they've been waiting for?"

A ripple of movement went through the

golden soldiers, and their unrest pursed Ariadne's lips. "Don't even try to turn them. They are loyal to me. They know I am meant to be their goddess."

"That was when they thought they had no other choice." I offered a fierce grin. "Now they have two of us to choose from. I wonder who they'd prefer? Psycho lady who thinks stealing is okay? Or me, sister to the oracle and a mighty warrior? Someone who isn't hated by everyone."

"Shut your mouth!" Ariadne clenched her fists. "You're just a witch. And an annoying one at that."

"Just?" I arched a brow. "Is that a challenge? Because if so, I accept. Take off this collar and let's see just who's the stronger of us." I smiled. "Let's show your precious army who's the best one for the job."

"Throw her in!" Ariadne screeched.

The soldiers flanking me hesitated.

Ariadne lost her shit. "I gave you an order. Obey!"

"You need to remove her collar first," one of them reminded.

Ariadne glared at the bracelet on her left wrist.

The one connected to me, I assumed. "Leave it on. She's too tricky."

The soldier glanced at the well before saying, "If we do that, we'll lose it. There aren't many left."

"It doesn't matter. Soon we won't need them," Ariadne insisted.

One of the women shyly lifted her hand and murmured, "My goddess. If I might."

"What?" snapped Ariadne.

"You must at least remove the bracelet lest the drain of magic by the well not be restricted to just the prisoner," the woman stated, wringing her hands.

"Why didn't you say that before?" grumbled Ariadne, removing the bracelet. She tossed it in the well to a few gasps.

Nothing happened, but I could see the woman who'd spoken huddled by the wall looking afraid. I had to wonder what else she knew that Ariadne had been ignoring.

The mad wannabe goddess turned her frosty gaze on me. "I think we've dallied long enough. I'd ask you for your last words, but I don't really care. So goodbye and thank you for your donation to my ascension. Throw her in."

Once the order registered with the soldiers flanking me, there wasn't much I could do. A firm grip on each arm ensured I got tossed into the pit. I plummeted, feeling my skin sizzle as the magic flooding the well tickled all of my nerve endings. Typhon had likened it to a ticking bomb, and yet passing through the dense magic, I didn't feel any pain. Not at first.

I did, however, lose my clothes. Fabric disintegrated, leaving me naked. Top, pants, shoes, undies, all gone, but even better...

The collar disappeared too!

My magic filled me with a rush, and the euphoria that was short-lived. I'd no sooner gained it than it got yanked from me. The well drank my power, already bloated and yet still thirsty for more.

It took everything and, unlike the collar, left me with an aching emptiness inside. It was gone. My magic. My ability. Leaving me less than ordinary as I plunged to my death.

The loser talk acted like a slap. I was Deino Grae. A sister. A witch. A bitch. And a vengeful one at that.

Was I going to let Ariadne win?

Would I leave Typhon to languish?

Would I really die ignobly smashed into pink sludge?

Like fuck.

Of course, not wanting to die didn't stop the fact the bottom of the pit was fast approaching. I spread my arms and legs starfish style to try and better control my dive, but it turned out I worried for nothing.

As I neared the end of my descent, the magic thickened, solidified in a way that slowed my fall. It got so sluggish that I flipped into a standing position and landed with barely a bend of my knees, although I did slide as my feet hit the pile of bones littering the bottom.

I grimaced as I realized I stood atop the stripped leftovers of those who'd been tossed in the well. Their remains were bereft of clothing, hair, and flesh, leaving only the skeleton. The many sized and shaped skulls indicated Ariadne hadn't been picky about who she had tossed in.

The molasses thickness of the magic made it hard to move. Each attempt at motion was a strain on my body. I took in the fact I appeared to be in a room.

Yes, I said room.

The well widened at the base, and I saw

shelves carved into the walls. Even a large, flat pallet-like area that reminded me of a bed. There was art on the walls that showed a man with a fishtail swimming with sharks and jellyfish. He carried a trident. Given this was Atlantis, it could only be Poseidon. Which made me wonder who the second god he'd fought with was.

An almost full pivot brought me in sight of a niche, fancier than the other shelves. Round with the edges intricately carved. Within the recess, an oddity sat. A lump of something dark, shriveled, definitely dead, and yet it emitted a tiny pulse. Just a flicker.

I should have ignored it and sought a way out, yet why bother? The bones indicated there was no escape. I would die, and given how my skin reddened, I got the impression it wouldn't be long as the thick magic appeared to want to disintegrate me cell by cell.

With no magic, no Spider-Man hands and feet, or any kind of climbing tools, I had no way to escape.

No hope.

The biggest skull left behind became a seat for my ass. I'd never seen a head this big. Had Ariadne tossed a titan down here? I wouldn't put it past her.

I lifted my hand and stared as a layer of skin vanished, leaving behind a pink layer. How many more until we got to the real meat of me? It didn't hurt, but would that remain true once the skin was gone? How could I watch?

*Don't give up.* I heard Frieda's voice and looked around.

Still alone.

*You have a destiny.*

"Tell that to the crazy bitch who tossed me down here," I muttered.

*You need to swallow.*

Swallow what? My pride? Cum?

*Idiot. Eat the heart.*

"What heart...oh." My gaze returned to the niche and the nasty chunk within. I eyed it with distaste. "I am not putting that in my mouth."

*It's the only way.*

The only way to what? Escape this well? Foil Ariadne? Hunh. Either of those were reason enough. I wrinkled my nose and grabbed the hunk of dried meat. The leathery texture of it did little to make me forget I held a desiccated organ.

And Frieda wanted me to eat it? I'd rather—

*Eat it if you want to live!* I could hear the impatience and sighed.

"I swear, this better not turn me into a vegan," I muttered and popped the nasty hunk into my mouth.

# 19

The moment I put that dried-out hunk of flesh in my mouth, my taste buds recoiled. Talk about gross. It didn't help I remained too aware I chewed something long dead.

My stomach twisted. The bitter and acrid taste made me want to retch. Instead, I chewed, chewed despite its toughness, chewed despite the grossness, chewed even as I watched the nails on my fingers turn soft and my knuckles flake, becoming red and raw.

I masticated faster and began to swallow, the dry chunks getting caught in my throat, making me gag. I wanted to spit it out. Instead, I forced it down and, despite my revulsion, noticed something interesting.

My skin stopped tingling. Even more promising, the decay of my flesh stopped. Maybe I wouldn't die cell by cell after all.

I swallowed the rest, and swore I felt it travelling down my gullet. If I lived, I really didn't want to see it when it came out the other end.

A wicked thirst and a dry mouth had me wishing for water. What I wouldn't give for a drink.

*Splash.* As if someone heard my wish, the trickle of water landing in a puddle had me whirling to see a basin filling with liquid. It took only a few strides before I cupped my hands and brought it to my lips. Cool and refreshing. The surprise fountain eased the pastiness of my tongue, and yet I remained parched.

My body craved something else.

"Is she dead? Can you see?" The shrill demand by Ariadne had me looking upward, the shaft I'd fallen down deep enough the top appeared as a tiny prick of light.

A blob leaned over the edge, the golden helm glinting. One of those who threw me down, trying to kill me.

Fucking asshole. My lips pursed. I wondered how he'd like to fall.

As if someone gave him a heave, the deusvenati suddenly fell in the well.

"Aah." The cry lasted only as long as his plummet then cut off abruptly, his armor crushing upon impact and doing nothing to protect the body within. Dead on arrival and I couldn't find any sympathy given what he'd done.

Too bad, not so fucking sad.

My thirst became an intense hunger, my stomach cramping, demanding sustenance, but I had no food.

The shelf by the basin suddenly held my favorite kind of pastry.

I frowned. I didn't usually eat sweets for a meal.

A bowl of pasta, still steaming, joined it.

I arched a brow. This was no coincidence. Something read my thoughts and was granting wishes. And for every wish that crossed my mind, my hunger intensified.

Coincidence? Or did this have to do with the chunk of flesh?

Suddenly, I was thrust into a vision. I could

tell because the dude wandering around wasn't here in truth, and he walked right through me.

A glance down at my body showed me transparent like a ghost.

I appeared to be in the chamber at the bottom of the well before it got covered in bones. The bed still held blankets, torn in spots, stained as well. The fountain barely trickled. The man living in here was huge. Giant-sized in height and width, but gaunt. His cheeks hollowed. His appearance unkempt.

The dude, wearing a robe, paced, tugging at his beard and mumbling, "Ungrateful. Cruel." He glanced up the shaft, and I craned to see that it appeared covered. "Using my reservoir as a trap. I should have never told them about the metal. Stupid. Stupid." He hit himself in the head over and over.

In that moment I understood. The deusvenati god hadn't been killed quickly. They'd let him rot in a tiny room that sapped his magic. Trapped him and let him die slowly while madness consumed him.

How horrifying. It made me think of Typhon and how hard he must have had to work to not lose his mind. But would he succeed a second time? I dreaded what it might do to him to be trapped again.

The former Atlantean god kept pacing. "They think they're so clever. They think they can live in the paradise I made and treat me like this!" He stopped as he shook a fist over his head. "No. I'm done. Time for them to reap what they've sown. The magic is almost all gone. Soon they'll see their mistake. But it will be too late." He chuckled, and as he whirled to stomp back through my ghostly body, I saw the madness in his eyes, but I didn't grasp his plan until he'd plunged a knife into his flesh.

I gasped and gagged a little as he sawed through his own flesh, not making a single sound. The cracking noise would have made me puke if I had a corporeal body.

A beating heart emerged, dripping silver blood. As the dying god placed it in the alcove, he whispered, "To my successor I leave thee." He paused as he slumped, the hole in his chest leaking heavily. "I leave thee my godhood and planet." On his last exhalation, he huffed, "Avenge me."

I snapped out of the vision and licked my lips. The thick magic in the air coated my tongue, and upon tasting it, I hummed. "Mmm." I didn't remember power tasting so good.

My stomach fluttered.

Could fulfilling the dying god's wish be so simple?

I opened my mouth and inhaled.

*Aaaah.* A rush of magic entered me and lit my body.

I sucked in even deeper the next time, feeling a euphoric rush.

More, I needed more!

I gulped at all the magic they'd been dumping in the hopes of bringing back their god. A god that was dead and now being digested in my belly. His heart, now a part of me, making me a part of something bigger. I didn't understand how the chamber that slowly drained him could contain all that arcane power.

It didn't matter, because suddenly all that magic became mine, and as it flowed into me, my body jolted and my eyes closed. A tsunami of sensations hit. A torrent of information too.

Memories, not all of them mine but ghostly remnants of those who'd died screamed past my consciousness. I might have gone mad except for the fact my mind filtered the emotions out of it and kept only the pertinent parts.

As my consciousness expanded so did my awareness of the world around me.

And I meant world.

Suddenly, I could see everything all at once. From above the planet swirled with dirty clouds. When the mucky winds parted, I could see once-pristine oceans, murky and lifeless. At least on the surface. Below, far below ocean and land, sparks struggled to survive.

Waiting for a god to guide them back into paradise.

A beautiful world ruined by the deusvenati.

God killers.

The reason I was in a pit.

Behind the death of everyone in Zuzamenn.

They helped Ariadne exile Typhon.

They and Ariadne had to pay.

With the magic all mine, I exploded upwards. I didn't need a spell or even a how-to lesson. Flying was just something I could do.

I emerged from the well and floated above it, taking in the surprised expression on Ariadne's face. The golden soldiers froze in place, the women and their younglings cowered, except for one child.

A little boy pointed and said, "Pretty goddess."

*Who, me?*

Before I could smile, a young girl lisped, "She's naked."

A glance down showed my body nude and glowing. A nice body, I should add, but not something I wanted to expose to anyone but my lover.

It took but a thought to clothe myself, my magic fabricating the perfect outfit. A dark ensemble fit for an angry sorceress.

Because I was smoking mad.

Ariadne gaped before yelling, "You stole my power!"

She drew my attention and my smirk. "I stole?" I laughed, and the timber of it shook the very walls of the cave. "I wouldn't speak, thief."

It took but a flick of my fingers to divest her of her last remaining armband, the one that had kept Typhon weak.

It fell away, and Ariadne screeched as she scrambled to grab it. When she would have slapped it back on, I turned it to dust. I don't know how. Just that I wanted it gone and so it obeyed. Good. Nasty artifacts.

Her mouth rounded. "This wasn't supposed to happen. You were supposed to die."

"I told you to not mess with me," I growled.

"Kill her!" Ariadne screamed. "Kill her before she kills us all."

The deusvenati looked undecided. Most stood there bouncing their gazes between me and Ariadne.

Only a pair chose to advance on me. I let them.

When one of them drew near enough to swing his sword, I grabbed it and squeezed, crumbling it.

The soldier recoiled, exclaiming, "Her magic isn't affected."

An interesting thing to say and a reminder the last god had been trapped by it. It appeared I was the new-and-improved version of deity. I smiled and beckoned. "Who's next?"

The other guard thought better of attacking, but I reached for him anyhow, grabbing his cuirass and lifting him. The golden shine turned dull before the armor cracked and fell apart, leaving behind a man with wide eyes and trembling lips.

"Forgive me, goddess," he blubbered.

"Not forgiven," I spat before tossing him into the hole. He'd been the other soldier to help throw me down there. Not a bad thing as it turned out, but his intent at the time hadn't been to do good.

As I turned my gaze back, the rest of the golden-armored hit their knees, and weapons clattered as they dropped them. Their heads hit the floor as they begged for mercy.

I had no interest in them or those cowering by the wall. I sought someone else but couldn't find her.

Ariadne had fled.

Unacceptable. I wasn't done with her yet.

No one stood in my way as I floated into the corridor. I didn't know which way Ariadne had gone, and yet instinct guided me. It led me to the portal room just as Ariadne prepared to step through an archway.

"Don't tell me you're leaving so soon. We're not done chatting," I purred.

I grabbed her in a fist of power and dragged her before me.

Ariadne should have been terrified. After all, I was using my nice voice, but she turned a visage twisted with vitriol in my direction and spat, "Cunt! The godhood was meant to be mine."

"No, it was meant for a woman from a banned world with the monster god's magic. Sounds like it was always meant to be me." I smiled, not very nicely I should add. "Now to decide how to kill you. Slowly, making you scream? Do I take my time and draw it out?"

"Let me go. You've won," she whined.

"Let you go? After what you did to those innocent folk in Zuzamenn? The way you came after me and my sisters?" I spat.

"Your sisters survived."

"The townsfolk didn't."

"I kept Typhon alive," was her shrill defense.

"And sent him to the place he hated most!" The reminder had me shoving her until she slammed into a wall.

She grunted, and I liked the huff of pain, so I slammed her again. And again.

The smell of her blood pleased me, as did her terror. About time she finally showed fear.

She wailed, "You can't kill me! I know how to get to Typhon."

I cocked my head. "You're lying."

Ariadne licked her lips. "No, I'm not."

"Yes, you are." I got close enough to put my face a mere inch from hers. "You destroyed the door, and the one on Earth is a decade away."

"There is another," she hastened to say.

"You've used it?"

"Not exactly. But I know where it is. I studied up on that place. Not easily either since it's been a while since people visited. It was called Apoleia, and while it's true that most of its doors were destroyed lest the monsters that thrived escape, there are still a few. And I know how to get to one of them."

I couldn't have explained how I knew she spoke the truth. "Tell me what you know."

"If I tell you, you'll kill me," she argued. "Keep me alive and I'll show you."

"You just want to trick me!" My magic grabbed her and tossed her across the room. She landed by the tunnel entrance.

She pushed herself to her feet. "I want to—"

"False god!" The yodel came from the soldier that suddenly appeared in the doorway. I didn't have time to stop the spear. He stabbed Ariadne in the heart, his aim true and fast enough she didn't have time to make a sound. She died before telling me what she knew.

Died before I could find out how to save Typhon.

"You idiot!" I screamed and lashed out. The lightning fried the soldier on the spot, and I didn't care.

Those tin-canned fuckers had pissed me off for the last time. Time for them all to die.

# 20

## Typhon

Typhon spent some time exploring the chamber he'd arrived in. Much like the one on Earth and old Atlantis, it held several doorways, all of them broken, including the one he'd just come through. He watched it crack and crumble as the deusvenati destroyed it from the other side, stomping all over his hope.

Hard to feel anything but intense rage as Ariadne once again trapped him. But worse? Knowing his witch remained alone, in dire danger, and there was nothing he could do to help.

"I should have said no." Should have never agreed to the foolish plan. If they couldn't prevail against the deusvenati in Zuzamenn, what made him think they could confront them in their world?

There would be time for regrets later. Now he had to survive if he ever wanted to escape here.

*What's the point?* Deino would most likely be dead within the next hour. Maybe less given how fast time ran in this place. Ariadne would either destroy Atlantis with all the wildly different magic she'd accumulated or actually ascend into true godhood. He'd still be powerless. No better than a mortal. No feasible way of getting his power back.

Insidious doubt crept in, slithering with its despairing logic. Had he fought this long and hard to give up now?

No. So long as he lived, he had to believe there was a chance to make things right.

It started with finding a way out of this world. Just in case he was mistaken, he tried each doorway, slapping his hand against the solid stone surfaces, getting increasingly agitated as each one failed.

It burned to know there'd actually been an escape all along. And he'd never found it. He'd searched every inch of the small continent he'd been stuck on. Walked the shoreline countless times. Climbed every hill. Explored every cave. But never found this chamber.

It could only mean he'd ended up on a different continent or island, one he'd never managed to reach. He didn't let himself dwell on the fact that if true, he couldn't even reach the original portal that opened every one hundred and forty-seven days.

There was only one exit from the chamber, and it wasn't long before he encountered his first obstacle: a cave-in that brought down part of the ceiling and blocked the passage. Not fully. There was a gap that took only a bit of work to widen enough he could slip past.

It wasn't the only impediment. A chasm required him running and leaping, throwing himself forward lest he fall down a deep hole he'd never be able to climb out of. On the other side, he found signs of life, small bones indicating something used this as a den.

He had no weapon and grimaced as he resorted to grabbing a rock. Never mind the fact that to use it he'd have to get close enough to bash. At least he wasn't empty-handed.

Daylight guided him out from the underground passage to a ledge high up on a mountain.

While he'd already known he'd not landed on the same oversized island as before, it still startled to see the vastness of the place. The familiarity hit him with a wallop that almost sent him to his knees.

The barren rocks. The stunted trees. The danger and death. It would be so easy to fling himself from up high and smash below. Which wouldn't kill him. Oh no. He'd suffer until something came along and tore him apart, finishing the job.

But then Ariadne would win.

That thought kept his determination burning bright as he began to clamber downward. His destination? What appeared to be ruins off to his left. Ruins might have answers. Some carvings that would explain more about this world. A map would be welcome.

Halfway down, a bugling noise drew his attention. He glanced over his shoulder to see a speck in the sky, heading for him. Wonderful. He clung to the rock face with his hands and feet. No ledge nearby for him to even try to stand and fight. The closest one was a twenty-foot drop below.

He didn't have a choice. He closed his eyes as

he pushed away and let himself plummet, the impact jolting even though he'd bent his knees when he landed.

A new cry from the sky had him rising immediately and grabbing the rock he'd put in his pocket. He scanned for the predator, and his jaw dropped.

This wasn't the smaller birds that used to inhabit the other isle. The massive size of it dwarfed him, and as he took in the features, he breathed, "Dragon."

Extinct on Earth with good reason. They were the apex monsters of that world. Wild and predatory. He'd done his best to try and protect them, as they were majestic and beautiful creatures, but they wouldn't leave the humans alone. He'd mourned when they went extinct.

It eyed him and saw food. Not the monster god. Not someone to fear. The rock in his hand would be useless. It fell from his fingers, and he raised them, pointing at the dragon. He pushed everything he had into a word of power.

*I command thee.*

But he remained too weak and drained from his earlier effort. The dragon didn't even pause at his puny effort.

The massive beast pulled up in front of his ledge and eyed him.

"Help me and I will find a way to reward you." He tried bargaining.

The creature hissed, and a long limb tipped in claws extended. There was no escaping its grasp. The dragon pinched Typhon in its talons and rose.

It flew higher and higher, high enough he knew better than to struggle. A fall from this height would leave him in pieces. They didn't soar for long. A wide ledge and a cave entrance showed their destination. Typhon got dropped and only barely rolled out of the way before the dragon landed.

Up close, the beast proved even more impressive, its scales seemingly black with a blue undertone. Its eyes were cold ice chips. It huffed, the steam of its breath smoking in tendrils. Its sinuous neck undulated as its head bobbed and weaved, getting closer and closer. Just like the dragons of Earth, it liked to play with its prey.

*I can't believe I'm going to end my life in the belly of a monster.* Ironic.

The dragon lashed out, once more grabbing hold of him, and this time, he did struggle, to no avail. To his surprise, the dragon used a claw on its other limb to tug at his collar. It refused to budge. The dragon uttered an annoyed sound as it lifted him to stare. As it eyed Typhon, its eyes glowed, bright with magic.

The collar fell off.

And nothing happened. His powers were a world away. Too far.

Typhon could have screamed with frustration. The dragon's maw opened, and Typhon could see into its mouth, the jagged teeth that would chew him.

The jolt that hit his body must have hurt because he got dropped. He jiggled as the magic that was his by right of godhood returned.

He got bigger, stronger, and suddenly he could feel again. Feel the monsters in this world.

The dragon hissed.

Typhon smiled. "You want to fight? Let's do this then." Time to show them all who was a god again.

# 21

My rage filled me. With Ariadne dead, I had no way to find Typhon unless I wanted to wait about ten years for the next eclipse. Would he last that long? How he must despair being trapped again in his prison.

And this was all the deusvenatis' fault. They did this. They could have neutralized Ariadne upon her arrival. Never listened to her bullshit. How about never should have created those collars? Not bad enough they'd ruined their world, they'd tried to spread their anti-arcane thinking.

No more.

I stalked through the tunnels, and if I saw golden armor, I pulverized it. But the random zaps weren't enough to appease. I found the chamber holding the well of sacrifice and collapsed it, the groaning of rock making the woman and children wail while the soldiers formed a line in front of them.

The little boy who called me pretty earlier whispered, "Goddess is mad."

Damned right I was! But even I drew the line at killing kids.

My fury had me exploding through the ceiling, pushing through tons of rock to emerge into the windy, dirty sky. The sun struggled to brighten through dense clouds.

Look what they'd done to this planet. Memories of it from before, given to me by the god I'd ingested, showed it as lush and bountiful. Its cities had been a meld of necessity with nature that only enhanced the beauty. All gone, a reminder of the deusvenatis' transgression.

Lightning crackled from me, zapping in all directions, making dark clouds even more somber, heavy with acidic moisture. I could have fixed the world. I knew how. Knew where to put a magic stopper to stem the poison spewing from under the crust. Filtering that toxicity was what the old gods used to do.

But the deusvenati didn't deserve it. They chose to betray their god.

*Betrayed me.*

As I floated above the mountain holding the cavern and a portion of their remaining civilization—with other pockets scattered in other tunnel systems—I was ready to murder them all. Which was when someone dared to interrupt.

"Goodness, what a temper tantrum. I knew I should have spanked you more as a child."

My mother's sudden voice interrupted me from meting out punishment. It took me a second to see her as a speck on the ground, standing below the hole I'd punched in the cave.

I dropped from my height that I might face her. "Mom? Is that really you?" I couldn't stop a suspicious lilt.

She looked different, even though it had been only a few weeks since I'd last seen her. The woman who'd raised me had ditched the hippy style. She wore a leather bustier that did amazing things to her breasts, snug britches showcasing her hourglass shape, and knee-high boots. Her hair remained long, but rather than hanging loose, she had braids twisting the front part out of her face. She also wore daggers on each hip.

"Yes, it's me, and before you ask for proof, remember the time you wanted to use my lipstick and I said no so instead you got the permanent marker from the drawer and colored your mouth green?"

I did remember. At five, I'd not been good at staying within the lines and had a clown-like smile for weeks.

"You survived." Last time I'd seen my mom, she'd gotten tossed into a dimensional rip.

"As if there was any doubt," she retorted with a snort.

I frowned. "How did you get here?"

"Same way as you. Through the Zuzamenn portal. It was quite the journey, too. The place Ariadne sent me proved challenging."

My lips pinched. "You shouldn't be here. It's not safe."

"Seems to me the real danger is gone. That is, if you can control your temper tantrum."

"I'll be pissed if I want. They deserve it," I spat.

"They're misguided, yes, but destroying the planet is extreme unless you want to be the shortest goddess to ever live."

"I never asked to be a goddess, and it's not like

they care about this planet." I glared at the huddled remnants of deusvenati. "They killed the original god. Then, when they realized they fucked up, they doubled down and started sacrificing anyone with magic."

"They made a mistake."

"A mistake!" I roared. "They tossed Typhon back into his prison and destroyed the way out."

"Ah. I see what this is about." Mother nodded. "You're worried about your lover."

"Yes," I hissed. "They fucked him. It seems only right I fuck them too."

"And how will massacring these people fix that?"

Logically I knew it wouldn't, but I muttered, "It won't. But it might make me feel better."

"It won't. Take it from someone who deals in betrayal. Vengeance isn't the answer. Not when you should be looking for ways to reach him instead."

"How? Ariadne died before she could tell me how to get there through another door." My lower lip jutted.

"Ariadne was a twit. Why look for a door when you have one right here?"

"It's broken," I reminded.

"So fix it."

"Oh, because that's so easy," was my sarcastic retort.

"You're a goddess now."

"And? So are you. Why don't you repair it?" Could she? My mother had been doing this god thing for longer than five minutes.

"I don't have your strength. Not all gods are made equal. My power is in betrayal. Yours, though…" She eyed me up and down. "It's an impressive mixture, but at its core, you have the heart of the original god of Atlantis, and he was all about innovation."

Her words left me pondering rather than angry. Could I fix the portal? Typhon had said something about them being around before he ever existed, but someone had to make them in the first place.

Mother coughed. "I don't suppose you could do something about the air. It's getting rather hard to breathe."

I'd not noticed, but at her mention, I saw the children wilting and coughing. While their parents might not be innocent, they were.

Dammit.

Once more I shot into the sky, and this time when I spread my arms, it was to do a few things.

One, I drew in the poison, which might kill living things but actually made me stronger. Apparently, I could filter it into power. That power could then be turned into a magical plug that I settled over the vent spewing toxicity into the atmosphere.

Next, I whirled, a mini tornado in the sky that twined and twisted the air, pulling it to me for further filtering. With the poison removed, the dust fell harmlessly to the ground. The winds died down, and as the clouds cleared, a ray of sun highlighted me as I floated back into the cavern.

As I alit, the deusvenati hit the ground on their knees, leaning over so their foreheads pressed against the floor as they chanted, "All hail the goddess. Bringer of the sun."

Hunh. I didn't hate the sound of that. Maybe they didn't all have to die.

Noise drew my attention to a tunnel and the voices that emerged from it.

It couldn't be...It sounded like...

People appeared, and I blinked, unable to believe my eyes.

"Frieda? Enyo?"

My sisters stood there, looking different but the same. Enyo had always had swagger, but now she had a style that enhanced her feminine side. Think sexy female Spartacus with a ginormous sword. Frieda, dressed in a tightly cinched robe and a wispy short-hair style, looked as if she could take on the world.

At their backs appeared three men. Bane, looking as grim as ever. John, still a golden pretty boy. But then there was Bacchus, looking thicker and healthier than when I'd last seen him. He tucked an arm around my mom's waist and gave me a nod and a gruff, "Good job."

What the fuck?

Movement at their feet turned into a trotting furball in chainmail. Not just any furball.

"Baby!" I screamed as I fell to my knees, arms open wide. My strutting dog might have looked impressive and tough, but the moment she laid eyes on me, her tongue lolled, and she galloped crookedly into my arms for a snuggle.

"What the fuck happened to you all?" I asked as I snuggled my face in Jinx's fur and got a tongue washing.

"We ended up in Tartarus," Enyo answered.

"Interesting place. It's where we found Mom and Bacchus. Sorry it took so long to get back."

"It's only been a few days," I murmured, still blown away my family was safe.

"Yeah, not for us. Think more like a few years. Hard ones," Enyo added with a dark glower. "Those Titans needed a few lessons on manners."

Sounded as if they'd had quite the adventure.

"Did you tell her?" Frieda asked, her question directed at Mom.

The goddess of betrayal fidgeted. "I was getting to it."

"Tell me what?"

Bacchus cleared his throat and offered a sheepish, "So it turns out I'm your father."

I stared. Long. Hard.

Mom squirmed a bit more. "I lied about your dad being human. And before you freak, Bacchus never knew. I kind of seduced him around the same time I stole that magic from Ariadne for the blessing."

I rubbed my forehead. "So we're the children of gods. Any other surprises?"

"Jinx is pregnant," Enyo blurted out.

I glanced at my furball with her tongue

hanging from her mouth. "Dare I ask by what, seeing as how you just came from Tartarus?"

Frieda clasped her hands together as she said, "Hellhound. But don't worry. I see her having a healthy litter."

Puppies? Okay, I was a little excited.

"Speaking of seeing, do you see Typhon in my future?" Might as well find out now.

"Yes. But you should hurry if you want to catch him at the right moment," Frieda added.

"Hurry she says. I still don't even know how to fix the fucking door."

"Stop whining and act like a goddess," Mom snapped.

I glared.

She gave me that look. The one that said don't be a twat. A familiar one from my youth.

"You and I are going to have a long talk about this, Mother," I muttered as I stalked for the portal room. No surprise, my family came along, as did Jinx, trotting by my side, leading the way.

I really wondered what kind of adventure led to my dog wearing armor. And getting with a hellhound?

Later. First, I had to stare uselessly at the

broken door. The freshness of the cracks made me clench my fists.

Fix it, Mom said. As if it were that simple. I wish I knew how to repair it. How to smooth the cracks.

The cracks disappeared as if the portal had never been broken.

Bacchus whistled. "She's got the power of creation. Nice."

I ran my hand over the stone. Pushed against it. "It's not working," I huffed angrily.

"Because you need to reconnect it," my mom chided. "Stop being so emotional and pay attention. Look beyond the door to fix its path."

"Look beyond, she says. Just fix it," I muttered.

I closed my eyes and tried to center myself. Bacchus called me a goddess of creation. Maybe I could wish the connection back into place.

Nothing happened.

My lips twisted. Why did this have to be so annoying? I just wanted to forge a path between here and the world Ariadne called Apoleia. It didn't even have to be permanent, just open a door long enough for me to slip through and find Typhon. If we got stuck there together until the next eclipse on Earth, so be it. At least he wouldn't be alone.

The stone under my fingertips hummed, and I opened my eyes to see it shimmer just like the other doorways. Had I done it?

"Want me to check the other side?" Enyo offered, unsheathing her big-ass sword.

"No. I'll go. Typhon is there because of me." Because I'd convinced him to come here.

"It's dangerous," Frieda remarked.

"Exactly. So don't you dare follow." A threat that I followed with a wall. A barrier between them and me, with me still by the portal. I wouldn't let them follow. This rescue was my responsibility. Mine alone.

I stepped into the doorway and out into a chamber much like the one I'd left. The doorways were broken but for the one I'd emerged from.

No Typhon, yet I sensed him. He'd recently passed through.

I followed the only exit out, noting the hole he'd made to get through a caved-in part of the passage. I floated over a chasm, my god powers following me here despite this not being my planet.

I emerged into pale daylight on a world that looked like it had been nuked.

Stark. Gray. Dead. I shivered at the sight. How had Typhon survived? I'd have gone mad for sure.

As I stared out over the landscape, I had to wonder where he'd gone. Once more my eyes shut, and I let myself simply feel, my body pivoting to give me a direction.

That way.

Rather than climb, I flew, standing upright and not horizontal like superman. I saw movement on the ground. Creatures that hunted. Pouncing and killing. A place that punished weakness.

A shadow overhead drew my attention, and I saw a giant, flying monster.

*Is that a fucking dragon?*

I gaped because, hello, ever since watching *Game of Thrones*, I'd longed to have one of my own.

It swooped for me, mouth opening wide, and it occurred to me I should probably do something.

"Halt." I held up my hand.

It ignored me and kept coming. Since I worried it might knock me from the sky, I dropped rapidly to the ground, wanting to be braced to fight.

I launched fireballs at it.

Lightning.

To no effect. Its scaled exterior repelled my efforts. Maybe I could wish it dead?

*Die, dragon.*

It kept coming for me. Apparently, my new godhood didn't allow me to control monsters.

Some rescue. I was about to be eaten five seconds after arriving.

*Sorry, Typhon. I've failed you again.*

## 22

## Typhon

Typhon felt her the moment she entered the world.

*What is Deino doing here?*

More shocking, she appeared to be coming from the direction he'd recently left.

He wheeled around, heading quickly for her, and spotted the glowing speck of her presence. More worrisome was the dragon arrowing in on her.

"Faster," he commanded the dragon on whose back he rode.

They dove to intercept the other beast, which pulled up when it noticed them coming.

His ride hovered before the other dragon, and Typhon boomed, "Touch her and die."

Basic as commands went, but effective. The monster chose to obey rather than be annihilated. The other dragon veered off, and Typhon landed his mount while Deino watched with an arched brow.

"And here I thought you needed rescuing," she accused.

"Jealous of my dragon?" he teased, sliding off its back.

"Very." She cocked her head. "You have your powers again."

His lips curved. "I do. It seems I'm not the only one who's changed. What happened?"

She waved a hand. "Got sacrificed but didn't die. Ate jerkied god-heart chased with a whole well of magic, and took out the twat causing us trouble."

"You're a goddess," he stated as he strode for her.

"Now who's jealous?" she taunted.

"You mistake me for a man who cares if a woman is stronger. I don't. In my time, only humans subjugated their females. Us gods, we celebrate power."

"Celebrate how?"

He dragged her into his arms for a kiss. A sound embrace that conveyed his relief and his affection.

She'd come for him.

Braved a monstrous world to find him.

And he never wanted to let her go.

Their lips meshed in a searing kiss that ignited. Their location might have lacked comfort, but in that moment, he didn't care. The monsters wouldn't dare attack while their god worshipped another.

Her body molded against his, and his arms wrapped around her, holding her tight as they kissed hungrily. The duel of their tongues kept them panting as magic stripped them naked but for their boots. Rough rocks on bare feet would have ruined the moment.

With her bared to him, he leaned back and cupped her breasts, squeezing their round weight, kneading them before he teased the nipples.

She moaned and shoved at him, pushing until his back pressed against a boulder. She crouched, grabbing hold of his erect cock and stroking it.

His hips jerked in time with her sliding grip,

and he just about lost it when she put her mouth on him.

He grunted as he held on. Not easy. She enflamed him with her touch. Aroused him just by being near.

She sucked, and his head went back as he strained to hold on. Enough. Pleasure shouldn't be one way.

He dragged her to her feet for a long kiss before swapping their spots. Now she rested against the boulder that he might drop to his knees in worship. Her thighs parted, and he nuzzled her mound as he lifted a leg over his shoulder, giving him full access.

His lips dragged on the soft skin of her inner thigh as he kissed his way to her sex. Wet and aromatic, the scent of her desire drove him wild.

She shuddered when he placed his first kiss on her nether lips. Moaned when he parted them with his tongue for the first lick. He lapped at her honey, a true desire for him, not because of power or fear. She truly did want him.

The first woman to do so with no ulterior motive.

Was it any wonder he wanted to worship her?

He licked and teased, toying with her sensitive

button. Flicking it over and over, rendering her breathing quite ragged.

She arched her hips and mewled, demanding more.

He thrust a finger into her channel. Felt her clench as he continued to lave her sweet spot, feeling her tighten.

"Fuck me," she huffed.

"Come for me," he demanded.

She grabbed his hair, and her hips bucked against his mouth. Her orgasm unleashed, the undulating waves making him unable to hold back any longer.

He stood and turned her around, her hands braced against the rock. She tilted her buttocks without him asking.

His cock aimed for the invitation, but he slid a hand around her hips to tease her first, waiting until she moaned and rocked her hips before he slid the tip in. The heat and tightness had him pausing. It wasn't their first time, and yet it might as well have been. Each sensation was intense.

Addictive.

Pleasurable.

He pushed into her, seating himself fully. Her

channel still quivered from her first orgasm, and he basked in the little pulses.

She wiggled and growled. "Stop teasing."

"As my goddess commands." He ground against her, not really pulling out. More like he rolled his cock to push deep. She keened as he butted against her inner sweet spot, tapping it over and over, her sex clenching so tight it was almost painful.

But the kind of pain that led to ecstasy.

He moved faster, his fingers digging into her hips as he kept grinding. Her gasps turned to halting moans, her body tightening.

When she came, he came with her. His bellow was almost as loud as her scream, a shockwave that rolled out from them and left them both breathless.

But satisfied.

When they separated, he turned to drag her close.

She rested her cheek on his chest and murmured, "Wow. I should rescue you more often."

"You do realize I was on my way to find you."

"How? The doorway was broken."

"I would have found another. I would have done anything to get back to you." He brushed his fingers against her cheek. "I worried I'd be too late."

"Would you have been upset?"

"Very."

"I almost ended the world when I thought you were lost forever," she confided with a shrug. "But my mom stopped me."

His brow lifted. "Your missing mother has returned?"

"Along with my sisters and my dog."

"Sounds like I missed quite the show."

As she relayed what happened after his expulsion, he found himself laughing even as he hugged her tight.

He'd almost lost her. Instead, everything turned out right. Ariadne died, and he had his powers back, which led to him grimacing.

"What's wrong?" she asked.

"It just occurs to me I have nothing to give you. I promised you immortality, but you achieved that on your own."

"Guess you'll have to give me something of equal or greater value then."

"Such as? You already have a planet to rule. As much power as me."

"There is one thing I don't have that you can

give me," she murmured as she drew him close for a kiss.

"What?"

"Your love."

He brushed a strand of hair from her cheek and offered her a cocky smile as he said, "You should have asked for more, because it's already yours."

For now, and forever.

# Epilogue

Being a goddess had its benefits—once I cleaned up my world and restored its first city along with its original name. Time to put Nullarcana and its atrocities in the past. Atlantis would dazzle with its beauty and innovation.

My new life involved a gorgeous castle by the sea, delicious food, no housework, and a closet that put my old one to shame. But all of that paled in comparison to the man sleeping in my bed.

My lover.

My god.

The stealer of dogs.

"Traitor," I muttered, eyeballing my furball cuddled on his chest.

## Gentleman and the Witch

Jinx had taken to following Typhon around with adoring eyes while, at the same time, being the perfect guard dog. No one could come near Typhon without my dog noticing and losing her shit. It didn't help that the first time someone tried to kick my dog—and died for it—Typhon had given the little brat the ability to transform from tiny lap puppy to giant, slavering, hairy, muscle-bound, saber-toothed hell-Pomeranian. Sounded funny until you got mauled by three hundred pounds of cuteness.

Still, it was hard to be too angry. After all, I did love the man, so I could totally understand.

For those wondering, Jinx had her litter of puppies not long after our reunion, and despite me wanting to keep them all, Jinx actually chose to give the three away once she weaned them. My sisters and mom each got one of the ugly mutts. Remember how I said my dog could transform? Yeah, her puppies came that way permanently. They started out small, but six months later, they were utterly terrifying—and adorable. They loved their auntie Dina, as Typhon always knew how to get the biggest and best meaty bones for me to spoil them with.

Speaking of the furballs, I'd be seeing them

tonight when they came to dinner. I wasn't the only one who chose to not return to Earth. As the new Oracle, Frieda found herself in too much demand and had asked to come live on one of my islands. I gave her a lovely one with a castle still being renovated on a bluff. My sister Enyo bounced between our places when she wasn't off with Bane, fighting other gods' wars.

My mom and Bacchus did return to Earth but visited often, our parents rekindling their love affair. Gross.

They were coming for dinner too.

"I don't suppose you want to come back to bed?" Typhon lounged, naked and tempting.

"And shower again? I just did my hair."

He arched a brow. "By snapping your fingers."

My lips curved. "Better than any hair straightener by far. Get your lazy god-monster butt moving. They're bringing the puppies."

"I swear, you love those dogs more than me," he grumbled.

"I do. Get over it."

I deserved the sudden slap on my ass and laughed. I did that often with him. He kept me balanced. And happy.

We were late to dinner because I did end up pouncing him one more time and had to do my hair again.

My sisters and mom were already gathered on the terrace, their giant puppies lying at their feet until they saw me.

Typhon grumbled as they bowled me over, as if the traitor had reason to complain, given he carried my dog tucked under his arm.

When I finally rose from the mess of furry bodies, I hugged my family. All together for the first time in what seemed like ages—a.k.a. two weeks. Used to be we couldn't go a few days. At times, I missed it.

As we prepared to sit, a sudden darkness fell. A glance overhead showed the two moons of Atlantis crossing over the sun. An eclipse. The first since I'd arrived and why I'd wanted a family dinner.

The shadow bands danced and tickled our skin. My stomach wrenched.

Blerg.

The triple projectile vomiting took everyone by surprise.

A good thing I had magic to clean us up quickly. Then I apologized. "Sorry about that. It must have been something I ate at lunch." And everyone knew if someone puked, everyone followed.

Frieda shook her head. "That wasn't bad seafood. Take another guess."

It took my husband shouting, "All hail the mother of monsters!" for me to smarten up.

"Holy shit," I gasped. "I'm pregnant." I glanced at my sisters. "We all are."

We eyed our bellies then each other.

"Did you see this?" I asked Frieda.

She offered a half-smile. "I see all kinds of things."

"Like?"

"A future of vast possibilities for the children of the Grae sisters."

And many adventures ahead.

THUS ENDS THE EPIC ADVENTURE. *I hope you enjoyed this series inspired by art. Once I saw the covers, I couldn't resist and had to write their story. Until we meet again in the pages of a book.*

**FIND MORE BOOKS AT EVELANGLAIS.COM**

www.ingramcontent.com/pod-product-compliance
Lightning Source LLC
LaVergne TN
LVHW031537060526
838200LV00056B/4539